Hello,
Good-bye

HELLO, GOOD-BYE

Lynn Klamkin

DODD, MEAD & COMPANY
New York

ISBN: 0-396-06782-4
Library of Congress Catalog Card Number: 72-12438
Printed in the United States of America
by Vail-Ballou Press, Inc., Binghamton, N. Y.

For Bernie

Fall
1968

She was very fat. I opened the closet to see what kind of a girl she was, and she was fat. I pulled out an imitation leather jumper and held the seam under the left arm in my hand and the only way I could hold the right seam at the same time was with my arms outstretched. She was probably a very gross person.

After choosing a progressive college, and anticipating what I would do with all the freedom and the excitement of meeting new and terribly creative people, the whole thing boiled down to roommates. That reduced me to a mortal level, which was all right, except that having such a sickeningly fat roommate made the idea disgustingly real. I had come to Vermont expecting to be liberated from the humdrum world of Watertown and all I got was a fat roommate who probably smelled and was going to major in math.

I tried not to think about it or at least think that there was some mistake and that my roommate was at least going to be superwoman or maybe a Joan Baez. Actually, I would have preferred to see another ordinary theater freak like myself, but no one, from what I saw in the registration line, seemed to fit the part. If my roommate couldn't be like me, I would like her to be unique. I mean, *I'm* unique, but in a sort of ordinary way.

The room itself wasn't too bad. On the second floor overlooking a pond that had a sign that said "Swim at your own risk." If you didn't look at the grass around the pond, it would be a lagoon out of the Tarzan series. If it wasn't Vermont, there would probably be alligators or at least piranhas. I started to unpack. I had forgotten that I packed so many sweaters and I realized almost immediately that there were not going to be that many fashion-conscious people at school who would even care what I was wearing. I was relieved that those Oh-what-a-neat-Villager-outfit days were over, but I was also afraid that someone would notice all of my Villager clothes and laugh.

People were starting to enter the dorm but no one came into my room. I peeked out of the door, nervously waiting for Kate Smith to come back to her room. God, how I already hated her. And where the hell was she anyway so that we could straighten out the who-gets-what-closet mess? I started to take inventory of her belongings. Not one, but two guitars. Fine. A Herbie Mann songbook. Awful. *Sixteen Famous Plays.* Not bad. A Max Factor make-up kit. Disgusting. A box containing a portable TV set. All right. I'll admit it. I'm glad she brought that. I could have brought one but I thought I'd be laughed out of school. Now she'll be laughed out. Records. Peter, Paul and Mary. A little old but okay. Complete Beatles record library. That I like. Herbie Mann—really!

So there was nothing left to do except wait or not wait. If I waited, I would meet *her.* If I didn't wait, I could go down the hall, across the hall, downstairs, to another dorm or to some other town and start meeting some people for a change. I flipped through *Sixteen Famous Plays* as I sat by the window. As I started reading *The Sea Gull,* I looked out of the window to the pavement. There was a very big shadow. I looked up a bit more and there was a very fat girl waving nervously to me. I suddenly panicked. This was the beginning of my four years in college and my roommate was not June Allyson. In fact, no one looked like June Allyson except for one boy I saw in the registration line. Was this disaster of a roommate in some way a prophesy on four years? Why *me?*

"Hullo."

"Hi."

"I guess that I'm your roommate," I said, with an amazing amount of cheer. "My name is Jane."

She wasn't smiling. She didn't even look at me carefully.

"My name is Debbie Goldman."

11

"Well . . . uh, when did you get here?"

"Last night. Uh, we stayed in Montpelier at the motel. My sister and my mother and father. They all came. But I registered this morning and have been here ever since. I've just been, uh, trying to find my, uh, counselor."

"Who is your counselor?"

"The Dean. Alan, uh, Walker. Mr. Walker is my counselor."

I continued to unpack. "Aren't you supposed to call him Alan? I mean, it says in the catalogue that teachers and students call each other by their first names and I'm sure that goes for the Dean."

"Who's your counselor?"

"I think they were putting me on but her name is Conchita. Did you meet her yet? Conchita Rodriguez?"

"No. I only met Alan."

"Who?"

"Alan Walker. The Dean. My counselor."

"Oh . . . well, I understand that we are supposed to see our counselors some time before dinner. Hey, where's the dining room, anyway?" She looked as if she'd know.

"Pretty far back in the woods. I'll show you tonight when we go to dinner."

Those were the words I dreaded. I quickly made excuses to get out of the room and went to find Conchita.

She opened the door to her office and took me by the hand before I said a word.

"You moost be Yane. Jes. Yane Pottman."

12

"Yes."

She looked like a fifty-year-old Spanish madam. Her hair was a black rat's nest and she wore a tight black jersey dress over her lumpy body. She stood up, but obviously uncomfortably. She was wearing high spike heels.

"Well, Yane, what do you wees to study here?"

"Drama. I really like drama. And, uh, psychology. I did some independent study in high school in child psychology. And I guess—I guess education. Maybe a language. I have taken both French and Spanish."

I was groping for courses after drama and I couldn't decide why I had to throw in that last thing about languages. My bullshitting days were supposed to be over.

"Well, youa yust take dese sleeps of paper and feel dem out after orentasun. Eet's bin nice to mit you, Yane. Eeef you wees to taka Espanees, le' me know."

College meatloaf is a lie. It is not made of meat at all. Mother's meatloaf has substance. College meatloaf has breadcrumbs and God only knows what else. The logical thing to do would be to smother it with ketchup, but college ketchup is watered down, so you are stuck.

Debbie sat next to me—or among me—while I ate and observed the new students at Laurencelle College. We ate in silence. I was busy trying to figure out what kind of a person goes to the most progressive college in the country and she was trying not to be self-conscious. I felt very sorry for both of us. God knows I didn't want to be identified so quickly as *her* roommate and she looked more than out of place wearing a woolen jumper in seventy-five-degree weather.

An old student stood up and started to bang on the table with a salt shaker.

"Okay, you freaks. Listen. There's gonna be a meeting tonight of all the new students in the dining room which is right here at seven o'clock."

I turned to Debbie, who was now slowly eating her chocolate pudding.

"How is it?" I asked.

"How's what?" she replied, not looking at me.

"The pudding. I don't eat that crap any more. I mean, I used to eat crap all the time but I stopped. I gain weight very easily."

"Oh?"

"Really, I do. . . . I was very, very fat all through high school and then last spring I just stopped eating a lot of crap like that and I lost thirty-five pounds. It changed my life."

"I think that I'll finish unpacking now."

She left very quickly and I knew what she was feeling all the time I was telling her about my diet. People used to do that to *me* all the time and it really hurt me a lot. But I couldn't stand to look at her because she reminded me of a rather miserable part of my life that I would just as soon forget. But I couldn't understand why I was deliberately trying to hurt her. I couldn't stand to be near her or with her.

I waited until she left and started the walk back to the dorm. I wished that there was an alternative to that but there weren't too many people clamoring to be with me on my first night at school.

As I walked out the door a very skinny boy pushed the door open for me. It wasn't gallant. He just seemed to be in a hurry to get somewhere. I walked quickly to keep up with him and he smiled shyly at me. Shyness was rather unusual at Laurencelle. I wanted to say hello or get lost or ask where he was from but I was really afraid of college for the first time in eighteen years. I had looked forward to going away from Watertown for so long, and now I was afraid that someone who was very possibly in the same position as I would spit on me if I said hello.

I arrived at the dorm and went up to my room. Debbie was seated at her desk and she looked out the window when I came in. She was writing in a little green book that looked all too much like a diary. Oh great. My roommate records everything that's going on. I can read it now: "My roommate gives me a pain in the ass . . . I wish that I were home . . . I miss my family . . . I hate college life and all the people who go to this crazy school . . . I have been here for six hours."

"Hey," I said, a little commandingly. "Where are you from?"

"New Jersey."

"Oh yeah? Where in New Jersey?"

"Just a few miles from Newark. Rahway."

I expected that she would at least ask where I was from or why I was at school but then I figured it out. She was very scared of me. I couldn't imagine that but I went on with the question-and-answer period.

"Have you got any brothers or sisters?"

"I have an older sister. She's twenty-three. She and I are very close. She's my best friend."

"I have an older sister. She's a bitch."

"How can you say that about an older sister? I mean, Carolyn is my very, very best friend in the world. How can you call your sister a bitch?" She seemed to get a little more excited.

"She just is," I started to say, until I decided that I had better give some explanation. "She completely lorded it over me for seventeen years until she went away to college. She and I are two different people. She was rah-rah and I was just . . . blah. I mean, not blah, but I was just interested in different things, but stupidly, I thought the life she led was fantastic and she kept telling me what a mess I was. She's very, very beautiful, you see, and always was the most popular kid at school and the whole bit. It's the story of the century, right? I mean, the older sister being out of *Seventeen* magazine and the kid sister being Georgy Girl. Well, the thing was that I wanted to be all the things that Sandy was, and I couldn't make it. I'd always run for things. I ran for . . . and in one year . . . Student Council President, and lost. I tried to succeed my sister and it was a joke. She supported my opponent.

"Then I ran for editor of the yearbook and lost. Then I ran for, in the following order, talent show chairman, prom chairman, senior treasurer, graduation program chairman, and finally wound up writing the class song. No one else would touch it. Well, when I did that, everyone loved it and on graduation everyone cried.

Everyone except Cliff and me. We wrote it together and we did a satire on class songs. It was a deliberate satire and everyone thought that it was fantastic. It goes to show you what the town was like where I live. People fall for people like Sandy. I finally told her to go to hell after she came home for Christmas vacation and told me what to wear when we were going out to dinner. I told her in no uncertain terms to go to hell. She just looked at me as if I had said nothing and continued to tell me what to wear. I think that was the bitchiest thing she's ever done to me. She couldn't give me the satisfaction of letting her know that I didn't need her to tell me what to wear."

"Punch her," the man shouted. "Just walk up to her and punch her in the stomach."

On the third day of school we were invited to attend a confrontation seminar with an angry young twit named Norman Beil. Now, let me explain. A confrontation to me has always meant showing my father my report card. Or it could be the time my mother caught me smoking in the bathroom when I was ten. But today, by Norman's description, it means that a demure-looking brunette was supposed to walk up to me and sock me in the stomach until my "guts fell out."

I blocked it. The punch, I mean. I didn't block the look that Norman gave me when I told him it was the silliest thing since Flavor Straws.

We talked for an hour or so about people spilling their guts in other ways . . . something that I noticed Laurencelle College students did with great talent and frequency.

"I hate my mother . . . I hate my father . . . I'm afraid of other students . . . I'm afraid of growing up . . . I'm afraid to face life . . I'm afraid someone will kill me."

"I'm afraid we're running out of time," Norman said, rubbing his eyes. "I ask only those of you who can take the punches to sign up for my confrontation course . . . only those of you who can take it as well as give it."

"That's a lot of crap," the brunette said to me. "I mean, it would be the easiest thing in the world just to sit for an hour and accuse everyone."

"Thanks for not killing me in there. He's some sort of sadistic idiot."

Her name was Leslie Shapiro. We walked into dinner together and decided to skip it . . . although as Leslie put it, "Meals are the social event of the day here. There's nothing else to do."

I was sitting in the lounge of my dorm, Milton House . . . although it was always referred to as "the one next to the swamp." It was the first time I had chanced the lounge alone. I didn't want Debbie with me. Not two nights in a row. I was reading the course list.

Javanese Gamelon—Mon., Tues., 2–5, John Undering
Studies in Schizophrenia—tba Marion Conrad Loveland
Chairman Mao and the New Left
"Hi."

It was the tall thin boy I saw on the way back from the dining room.

"Hi," I answered, putting the course list down.

"Mind if I steal a cigarette?" He spoke very quickly.

"They're not mine. I don't. . . ."

"How do you like it here?"

"Fine."

"What are you here to study?"

"Theater. You?"

"Yeah. Me, too. Acting. God, it's great to meet someone who isn't planning to start a revolution or something."

For the first time in two days I felt comfortable. We had both gotten into the theater workshop. It was disappointing because we were both told how exclusive it was.

"God . . . I'm Roger. Roger Goldenson. I'm from Chicago. That's all the dumb stuff."

"I'm Jane Potterman. From Watertown."

"Where's that?"

"Connecticut."

"Oh."

"Look, I know everyone here is from New York or Boston or something. I'm the token hick. I thought there'd be people worse off than me. You know, from towns that are named after trees. Like Elm Grove, Oak Park, Maple Syrup . . . that sort of thing."

A very small, very pale boy walked in.

"Roger," he shrieked. "I've been looking all over for you."

His voice was incredibly high and every fourth word

seemed italicized.

"Jane, my roommate, Kirkland Chapin."

"Very pleased to meet you." He shook my hand. What a bony awful weak hand he had. The body, the voice, the weak hand . . . all were perfect for the character. Of what?

I continued my story to Roger.

"So, I come from a little nothing place. And you know what the big event of the year is? It's the Miss Watertown Pageant. Every year they get all these horrible girls together, either Polish or Italian, and the Chamber of Commerce does this whole pageant routine. And for the talent thing each one of them sings 'I Enjoy Being a Girl' for about one and a half bars and then breaks into this godawful tapdance. And let me tell you, the crowd goes apeshit over all of this and then gives the award. It was Sheila Szimerowski last year. She got pregnant."

"She should have kept tapdancing. She couldn't have gotten pregnant that way." It was the high voice that spoke up.

I laughed and sank back in the chair. The three of us laughed our way through the next two hours.

"I'm scared," Kirkland said to me after Roger left. "That's why I came over here looking for Roger. My stomach is killing me."

People were beginning to come into the lounge. I suggested we go into the hallway and, once there, under the staircase.

I told him that I used to work for a doctor and he

trusted me.

"Maybe it's nerves," I suggested.

"Yeah," he said. "I haven't been exactly Perry Como since I got here."

"That's a really terrific ring," I said.

"Thank you. It's lapis. I have to admit I really love it. I like your ring, too."

"It's an antique Wedgwood medallion, even though it's so tiny. It's valuable because it's got more than two colors in it. Most Wedgwood doesn't."

"I know. I saw a terrific urn at the National Gallery that was three-color."

"Do you like antiques?"

"Yeah. But not to possess them, not to *have* them. I like to see them and to think about what *they've* seen."

"Oh God, yes," I said. "My mother is so damned possessive about all of her antiques. 'Don't play near it. Don't touch.' "

"Me too."

"But the tiny things you find. I don't know. They're only special if there's a reason for them to *be* special . . . like this other ring here. It's just a little silver nothing. But I found it in one of the gardens at the Cloisters in New York. Sometimes I can look at the ring and remember everything . . . the gardens and the flowers, spring flowers, and the Hudson and the dress I was wearing and the brightness of the sun and where it was in the sky. And also the boy I was with, Clifford Filipowski."

"You don't sound as if you come from a hick town."

I was pleased to hear that.

"Do you like drawings?" he asked.

"Whose?"

"Mine?"

"Probably. I'm not a very great judge."

"You would be," Kirkland said. "I'd like to show you my work some time. If you'd like. I daresay I'm not Picasso, but maybe you'd like to see them."

I made all kinds of enthusiastic gestures, thinking all the time "daresay"? Who the hell says *that* any more?

During the time that I had spent at Laurencelle, three days, all I heard was "Communicate! Communicate!" And as I sat on my desk, overlooking the "swamp," I did want to communicate. But not to *them*. I wanted to write an open letter to everyone at Watertown High stating simply that this is me. At Laurencelle. And I am happy. And I am witty and I am bright. And young. And fuck you all. No. Not fuck you all. See? I am also forgiving.

But not really too compassionate. For only a few feet away was Debbie. She was propped up in bed in the middle of the afternoon, consumed by loneliness. She poured out her depression into her little green diary.

Our conversation was merely civil, and I always had to start it. Was she happy? Yes. Did she miss her family? Very much. Did she like movies? Yes. What else does she like to do? She can play the guitar, knit, sew, weave, and cook (obviously).

The dialogue ran for about three minutes and then I'd stare out of the window into the bright sunlight, into the tall green pines and away from all the people.

*　　*　　*

"I never show these to anyone," Kirkland announced as he unlocked his desk drawer and pulled out what seemed like an endless number of sketch pads.

"Wow!" I said. "I guess I don't have to ask you to account for the past eighteen years of *your* life."

"Tell me what you think."

The hours passed and we discussed every piece of work he had. Tiny economical pen-and-ink drawings. Just lines. Just brilliant. I really and truly fell in love with that. I loved that talent, that great gift. And he loved my appreciation of it. I knew that a one-line drawing was Bette Davis' hat in *Dark Victory* and he couldn't believe it. It was funny that movie and television trivia were becoming a basis of communication between us. I don't know why. It made everything sort of special—or "in."

"Incredible," he said.

"What is?"

"That you understand everything so well."

"Like what?"

"Like my work. My mother thinks it's *shit*."

"It's not. It's brilliant, Kirk. It really is."

"Thank you. But please do me a favor? Don't ever call me 'Kirk.' I just hate that."

"People really call you Kirkland?"

"Yes."

"Not Kirk?"

"No."

"Even when you were a baby?"

23

"They called me Pal."

"But that's a *dog's* name."

He was bruised by that. Visibly upset. On a ten-point scale of Visible Upset he was a nine. I quickly changed the subject.

"Your mother really thinks it's all shit, huh?"

"I don't want to talk about it right now. I mean, I will, but my stomach hurts. What I'd rather do is play some double solitaire. Do you know how?"

"No."

"I'll teach you, m'dear."

Preshrunk (pre-Laurencelle) always meant to me that you could buy a dress that wouldn't shrink after you washed it.

Wrong. It means that you've been through four to six years of analysis before you go to college. And just like the dress, you wear the label on your sleeve. Everything on the label was erased (Altman's, Lord & Taylor, Brooks Brothers) except for Preshrunk. It was somehow indelible.

But I was not. I was only Dacron and cotton. Period. Fully washable, tumble dry. Permanent press, drip-dry, wear-dated.

When I was in my early teens, I didn't plan it that way. I would go into periodic fits, stare at myself in the mirror, think about suicide, becoming famous, and maybe having some disease and six months to live. (Oh, wouldn't *they* be sorry!)

I always thought I'd secretly see a psychiatrist. I had no money and I thought I'd ask for a scholarship on account of being so deserving and all. But I never did. I didn't do it because I was afraid I'd find out I was normal. He'd say that and it would be like Bette Davis reading George Brent's "prognosis: negative." It would be worse than that. So I suffered alone. My mother sending me off to dances. My protesting. Oh, the whole schtick.

So, obviously, all these preshrunks at school had a whole different way of communicating with one another. "You're projecting. . . ." "You're internalizing. . . ." "That's very healthy of you. . . ."

Worst of all was having to sit among a group of preshrunks and listen to them talk about their therapy. Therapy cured them of everything but discussing their therapy.

So, although we had just met a couple of days after school started, it came as no surprise that Kirkland had been in analysis for four years. With Dr. McLeod in Washington. And he was not sure Kirkland could adjust to college, let alone Laurencelle. And the more Kirkland discussed his problems with me, the more I could identify with Dr. McLeod's problems, not Kirkland's.

To clarify any doubt, there is an academic side to all of this, and after the first month of classes I knew it. Here I was, Jane Potterman . . . college student. . . .

Now what is involved in being a college student at Laurencelle College? First, you must be one of the following.

1. An extremely intelligent, hardworking, well-informed STUDENT.

2. A potentially great student who cannot perform to his fullest capabilities until:

> (a) he straightens out his mess with his parents;
>
> (b) decides where to direct his enormous and diverse talent;
>
> (c) learns to read and write.

3. A good liar.

This obviously covers all territory. A spaced-out drug freak can claim No. 2 when cornered by a "concerned" teacher. A Laurencelle teacher does not get pissed-off by a lousy student . . . only concerned. An ill-informed nebbish can claim anything short of a runny nose as an excuse for not having done any work and not have so much as an eyebrow raised by any member of the faculty.

Take for example my *Modern Problems in Psychology* class.

Teacher: Marion Loveland. (A sixty-year-old mother with a capital M whose concerns and maternal instincts run as endlessly as her varicose veins.)

Class meets Mon. and Wed., 1:30 to 3:20.

It was an enormous class. Eighteen students. Marion claimed she was elated by our enthusiasm.

"I'm with you people," she'd often say. And she was . . . to the point of a breakdown.

We had dozens of books on our reading list. ("Only suggested," said Marion. "I *trust* you!") Anyway, there was one, *The Adjusted American,* which was required for a discussion in late October.

It was a short book and I read it. Not thoroughly, not in a state of awe and wonder, not even carefully. I finished it at lunch just before the class began.

Leslie sat next to me. Everyone thumbed nervously through their books and I knew they hadn't read it.

"Shall we begin?" asked Marion, smiling anxiously.

A two-minute silence followed. A few people fumbled for cigarettes and matches. A few had had the foresight to get stoned during lunch and were staring at various people, toes, trees, and ceilings.

"Well," continued Marion, only slightly flustered. "Who would like to start off with the author's description of 'autonomy'?"

In the next moments our eminent instructor, one of the original members of the faculty at Laurencelle (no kidding!), paled considerably. She caught herself suddenly and straightened up in the chair, crossed her legs, and went on.

"Now you people aren't usually this shy. How about starting off for us, Ian?"

Ian had started off about six hours before with a gram of hash. Wise up, Marion, I thought.

"Didn't you read the book, Ian?"

"Uh-uh."

"And why not, dear? Did you forget it was due?"

"Yeah, that's it."

"How about you, Sandra?"

"What?"

"Autonomy."

"Oh, yeah," Sandy Finkelstein said, playing with her Afro-Jewish hairdo. "I forgot."

"First chapter."

"I dunno. To tell you the truth, I didn't read it."

Sandy continued to explain that she *started* to read it, but her roommate was going to commit suicide, so she stayed up all night, talking her out of it. Marion asked forgiveness.

John Crimmins lost his book. (Aw, c'mon, Jack. That went out in sixth grade.)

Ruth Van Rand had to fly to New York for her best friend's wedding.

Maureen Hogan had to attend her best friend's abortion.

There were assorted forgetters, shruggers, book-losers, and even one out-and-out confession of not having bothered to read the damned book.

Then me.

"Autonomy?" I asked, just to get back to the original question. "Well—"

From that I went into my own interpretation of the author's theory of American autonomy. I took it point by point, occasionally answering Marion's questions, which were asked with total disbelief that I had read the book.

I had read it. So sue me.

There was no Goody Two-Shoes crap about my having read the book. Marion never congratulated me. She shouldn't have. I was supposed to have read it. Most of the kids were too stoned to care who had read it.

This was Laurencelle. Institution designed to foster academic freedom, freedom to express oneself, freedom from grades, freedom of choice (except in the dining room), social freedom, and freedom to accept or reject responsibility. So, this incident was of very little consequence because we were so *honest* about it.

But I still hoped that Marion would remember that way back at the beginning of the semester *I* was the one who had done the work.

At the beginning Kirkland said a lot of the things I was thinking . . . while I was thinking them.

"Freaks," he said. "Goddam crazy, crazy people. All they do is eat and fuck!"

"Yeah."

"And they don't love each other or anything. . . . You want to learn a secret?"

"Yeah."

"I'm a virgin."

I wasn't surprised. I couldn't imagine the situation being otherwise.

"Me too," I said.

"I had platonic relationships with a lot of girls before. But here you hear all the euphemisms for making love. Fucking, balling, screwing. . . ."

"And none of them really means 'making love,' which is kind of sacred."

"Exactly," he said. "Like, do you know Rhoda and Marshall who're in my poetry class? Well, she's the sultry bitch with long stringy black hair and he has the warts on his hands?"

I nodded.

"Well, all the poems they write are about the things

they do in bed. You know, 'Ode to my Erection,' stuff like that. It's revolting they don't love each other."

"Yeah."

"Whaddya want to be?" Kirkland asked me after we'd exhausted the subject of being at Laurencelle.

"You mean, when I grow up?" I asked.

"When you get out of here?"

I thought for a second. Then I looked at him and answered in one word. "Ept."

"Ept?" he asked. "What in hell is *that*?"

"It's the opposite of inept, which is what I am."

"How are you inept?" he asked. "I mean, you're not going to make me believe that."

"I can't do anything. Name something. I can't shuffle cards. I mean, I can't put a battery in a flashlight. I can't eat a tunafish sandwich without all of the tunafish falling in my lap. I was thrown out of three different dancing schools."

"Inept."

"Yeah."

Kirkland came to my room one night after dinner to watch *Casablanca* on Debbie's television set. It was fall. Full-fledged fall. We had picked up leaves on the way to my dorm and thrown them at each other.

"This is an abortion!" Kirkland shrieked.

"Yeah. They cut out Peter Lorre."

We continued to watch it. Then right at the beginning of "As Time Goes By" I felt Kirkland's arm around me. I looked at his face. It was tense and flushed, so I relaxed. He had that "should I or shouldn't I" look on his face. The whole damned campus sleeps with strangers night after night and he feels guilty or worried about having his arm around me.

The movie was finished and I turned off the TV.

"It was a real abortion."

"Let's make some popcorn."

"I've got a poetry class at eight-thirty."

"Okay," I said. "You'd better get going."

I walked him to the door.

"May I kiss you good night?"

"It's a Mickey Rooney movie!" I laughed.

He kissed my cheek and ran down the stairs. Presumably Lewis Stone would be there, telling him what to do next.

It's time I talked about myself. I *always* talk about myself. If I'm not talking about myself, I am usually at least thinking about myself. I don't know why.

Physically, almost everything's wrong. I don't want to talk about that. I never really look attractive. I'm used to it.

Once I really looked very beautiful. It was a once-in-a-lifetime thing. It was my senior prom. (I'll continue unless you're too hysterical thinking of me at a senior prom.) Miraculously, Clifford Filipowski asked me. I really liked Clifford Filipowski. We wrote the class song together and we were good friends. So we went to the prom together and afterward to the Womogo Inn for Chicken Maryland.

I bought a beautiful dress . . . yellow and very unusual and quite feminine for me. My hair was perfect. Long tendrils that were unglued, unlike everyone else's. I struggled all evening with contact lenses that I'd had for two years and that never fit right. Make-up, tall, thin, smiling and, as my grandmother put it, "A regulah Pygmalion."

Clifford Filipowski arrived on time, shyly handing me a bouquet of daisies. His eyes lit up and I could tell how much he enjoyed looking at me . . . the only time that had ever happened.

We arrived at the high-school gym on time. I watched the chiffon gowns and bunny furs before me. I remember wondering if all those bunny furs would multiply before the evening was over.

Then Clifford gritted his teeth and asked me to dance. He knew from experience that dancing with me might get him a draft deferment for smashed feet, but he was quite a polite boy. So we danced through the prom and through Chicken Maryland, and except for my contacts killing me I had a wonderful time. Cinderella story, right?

Three weeks later Clifford arrived at my house with the pictures that were taken at the prom. Him in his white dinner jacket, holding my waist. The phony fountain in the background. Hair, lovely. Gown, perfect. Bra strap, hanging down below my sleeve!

Drama class was my favorite. I think I'm an actress. You know some people walk up to an easel and can turn a canvas into a work of art. They take their paints and brushes and poof! It's ooh and aah time. The same goes for roller skates, piano, toe shoes, marbles, and even, I suppose, the accordion. But an actor has to step inside *himself*. He has to turn himself inside out like a pullover sweater.

Let me give you a brief résumé:

Jane Potterman, age eighteen
Previous experience:
1. Fifth grade: Mrs. Shoemaker in class production of *The Shoemaker and the Elves*.
2. Sixth grade: Understudy to Mary and angel in class Christmas pageant.
3. High school: summer of sophomore year, studied and worked at Haverton Playhouse. It was here that the actress learned to crosshatch while painting a set, first learned the meaning of the word faggot by observing her dance and music instructors, and learned to cry on cue.
Credits include: Chorus in *Bye, Bye, Birdie*, Nancy Gear (the star!) in *Young and Fair*, and a tambourine player in Lorca's *Blood Wedding*.
4. Summer of junior year: Although the actress became suddenly ugly that summer, she worked at Stoningham Playhouse (lived at home). She did more crosshatching, prompted the girlfriend of the boy she had a crush on, sewed eleven togas for a production of *Antony and Cleopatra*, and played half a whale (guess which half) in a Saturday-morning production of *Pinocchio*.

Also, somewhere in between all of this the actress screamed her way through the lead in a high-school production of *Sorry, Wrong Number.*

So, I mean, acting wasn't just a whim of my first semester. It was something I loved and something no one else in Watertown had discovered. The summers I went off to stock I was lifted above everyone and then would come back to high school again and resume my most difficult role.

Drama class at Laurencelle wasn't stardom. It was mime. "Pretend you're a flower closing up." "Count to ten and breathe along the horizon!" "Put all of your attention on your feet." Touch, feel, look, smell.

Rico Vega was a fortyish Greek god. Maybe not Greek, but certainly godlike. He didn't walk, he floated. He never angered. He never really laughed, although his manner was always pleasant. Really, it was as if he just did this favor three times a week for Alan Walker and descended from the heavens to teach a class. Then he floated back to Zeus.

And we, the mortals, adored him. Yet, I was never conscious of the "we" (Frankie Adams be damned!). Much of the class involved meditation. We would run off into the cool green meadows behind the campus and sit, lotus position, in a spot "where you feel most comfortable. Make the earth under you your home."

And so I did . . . meditate. Feel the sun, feel the earth move, feel the trees, feel guilty about spending four thousand dollars a year meditating.

"Man," a freak said quietly, "this is a natural high."

Then Rico instructed us to come together . . . all
ten of us. All strangers. And on the count of ten we
were to get closer . . . then closer . . . and finally become one. Then he clapped his hands and we were to
run far away until we landed in a spot we liked. Then
we were to call out words, sentences, anything, to each
other.

"Hi!"

"Hi!"

"You up there . . . can you dig this?"

"Yeah . . . groovy!"

A laugh.

"Yodel lo a lay hee hoooo!"

"Yodel lo a lay hee hoooo!"

More laughter.

"Hey you down there."

I looked up.

"You down there in the green sweater. Hey, I think
I love you . . . I mean, I kinda dig your face."

"Thank you," I said quietly . . . then screamed,
"THANK YOU!"

"Will I see you after dinner?" Kirkland blotted the
grease from his veal cutlet.

"Yeah, sure," I said.

"My room is filthy, but Roger will be out at a dance.
Oh, yeah. And my mother sent me some Toblerone that
I want you to try."

He was on the back stairs of his dorm, Conlon House,
waiting for me. He walked me to his room, which he

locked (he always locked his room), and I looked around to see if anyone in the hall noticed me going into his room. Not that I certainly didn't have to worry about any trouble as a result, but it's such an announcement.

"Can I offer you anything?" he asked.

"A Kleenex and a comb, please."

"Here's a handkerchief I got in Italy and a bamboo comb from Japan."

"But I just want to blow my nose and pull my hair back."

"Better not blow on the handkerchief. I mean, it cost a lot. Oh, and the comb's kind of fragile too."

I slurped and let my hair fall in my face.

"Oh Jesus! Dear God!" Kirkland clutched at his stomach.

"I thought you weren't religious."

"Very funny. I'm in pain. Oh God! My stomach! It was that dinner. Oh God! I must lie down. Can you take my pulse?"

"Yes," I lied. I held his wrist and looked at his watch.

"Perfectly normal. Look, maybe I'll call the infirmary. They'll help you."

"No. No. I don't think so. Just sit here and talk. No, we can't talk. This might be serious. Oh God, I hope not."

I ruled out appendicitis, beriberi, advanced pregnancy, cerebral hemorrhage, polio, and the vapors.

"There," he said, after a long silent pause. "It's a little better now. Maybe I should get some sleep and I'll feel better in the morning."

I unlocked the door and he sat up in bed, thanked me, and fell back. I looked out into the hall. It was empty and I left.

I had the feeling during those first few weeks as summer faded into a deep and beautiful autumn that someone was going to find out about it. I felt as if I belonged to a tribe of very savage people hiding over the next hill and someday soon a missionary . . . a cavalry of middle-class mothers and fathers . . . a whole society would hit Laurencelle and massacre the place. And, curiously, we wouldn't fight back. All these young radicals would fight with their mouths. And we'd win. We'd confuse the enemy to death. That is, if we didn't bore each other into submission in the meantime.

And so I wandered around, from class to class, person to person, looking for something durable. My mail supplied nothing. Family news. Smith is wonderful. Harvard's difficult. She's dating a Yalie. He's turning on and having sex with a Chinese girl from Radcliffe. But I was freer, happier, and clearly changing.

No longer was I shocked by the news of someone dropping acid. No longer was any little part of me silently condemning a couple who were living together. No longer did wild screaming, crazy clothes, or the smell of marijuana confuse or bother me. My mind was initiated. But I was clearly not one of the tribe.

Oddly enough, it didn't matter. No one really looked twice at me, either. No fingers wagged. No one dared me to do anything I'd never done. No one made me feel like a creep for not conforming. Remember when you were a kid and your mother-teacher-old maiden aunt (choose one) said you must have the courage to be an individual? I used to imagine being tortured into relenting to drink beer before I was twenty-one. But there was no pressure to do anything. I was being left alone. Alone, but with friends. Leslie, Roger, Kirkland.

And I felt, really, for the first time in my life, that I belonged.

The only time I had any real conversation with Debbie was when she was packing. I would watch her stuff a few dresses, her wig, and make-up into a hatbox. It all looked like a thirties movie.

"Where are you going?"

"New Jersey."

"When will you be back?"

"In a few days."

"Special occasion?"

"No."

The she would disappear. As soon as she was out of the room, I would pick up the little green diary. She left it right on her desk. I figured she wanted me to read it.

Dear Diary,

It is getting colder although my mother says that it is like summer in New Jersey. Up here we have already had one frost.

Why did I come here? I knew I wouldn't fit in and yet I wanted to prove that I could. I feel so awkward around people like Jane. Damn that bitch!

She is truly making my life miserable. What a pig. Who the hell does she think she is, anyway?

There is a boy in my Small Groups Workshop. His name is Eric. He is so handsome that I can hardly stand it. If only I could speak to him. If only, if only— He wears an embroidered shirt with flowers but he doesn't look unmasculine. He's so sensitive. What if he talked to me???

Meanwhile, I am going to New Jersey this weekend where I feel safe.

D.

It came to pass that I became known in some circles as Kirkland's girlfriend. At Watertown High it was always "the sister of Sandy" or the "fat bespectacled nobody on the debate team." Now I was somebody's girlfriend and I became very content with that. To tell you the truth, I liked him.

About the third week of school I saw Roger one night at dinner and I asked where Kirkland was.

The story:

Kirkland had opened a can of Campbell's beef and barley soup at four in the afternoon. About one minute later he had managed to lick some beef off the lid of the can. At four-oh-two he had decided he had contracted botulism and now, one half-hour later, after the deadly can of soup had been opened, he was sitting in his room, hysterical and waiting out the rest of his life, which, he was convinced, would last about two more hours.

"Kirkland."

"What?"

"May I come in?"

Sniffle. "Yes."

"What's the matter?"

"I'm going to die."

"Bullshit."

"Stop it! I have botulism. I'm poisoned, for Crissake! I'm going to die!"

"Look. From what I know about botulism, which I'll admit isn't a hell of a lot, I know that you die right away. Stop crying."

"I'm sure you can take your time with it. I swear to God I'm going to be dead by midnight."

"There's a movie tonight. Let's go."

"What is it?"

"*Virgin Spring*."

"Stop that!"

"I'm not kidding."

"I've got to call Dr. McLeod. He'll calm me down. God . . . wait. He goes to his weekend place in Chevy Chase on Fridays. Goddamn. I'll call a psychiatrist here."

"There are no psychiatrists here."

"I'll call a surgeon."

"Internist."

"God, I can't think. I'm going to die."

I sat down next to him on his bed and put my hand on his shoulder. He turned his head and continued to sob.

"Look, I might really go crazy myself except for one little thing. You're not going to die. Maybe you'd like to die so that no one would bug you, but you'll have to

40

think of something better than Campbell's soup . . . although you get my admiration for creativity. How about slitting your wrists? That's messy and you couldn't do it, anyway. You don't have a razor."

"Bitch."

"What the hell is bothering you? The first night you were here you had a stomach ache. You're always nauseous or something. You always try to make yourself sick."

"I do not. Do you think I like being sick?"

"No. I think you don't like being you."

"I've already had four years of analysis, thank you."

"Look. I'm really very, very sorry, but you are not going to die tonight unless you take some immediate and drastic action. I just would not count on the beef and barley soup, that's all."

"What should I do?"

"Either make out a will or go to the goddamn movie."

"Oh, great, Potterman. *That's* sympathy."

"That's constructive."

He moaned, "What am I going to *do?*"

"Well, if you make out a will, I want the red kimono. If you're going to the movie, get dressed."

He stood up and looked plaintively out the window.

"It's those *people*," he whined. "They can't accept me."

"You can't accept *them*."

"I can't think about it. I'm going to die."

"Must you *announce* everything before you do it? You know what, Kirkland? If you don't announce everything before you do it, you *ask* me. Jesus, you really are

41

insecure. What the hell is it? Are you afraid that your parents hate you? That some freaked-out black kid is going to rape you? That you'll lose all those—those *things* you brought with you to school? That you are impotent? That I'm going to tear up your drawings some night when you are asleep? Are you afraid that underneath the red kimono or the Chilean fisherman's poncho Kirkland Chapin is just as ordinary as anyone else on this campus?"

He quivered. He was sitting next to me on the bed and he was sobbing.

"Hell, Kirk, even if you got dropped from the Mensa Society, you'd still be *you*. It's those fucking labels that you attach to yourself. You need them, but they're gonna kill you."

"What labels?"

" 'Unwanted child.' 'Boy genius.' 'Junior victim.' "

He continued to cry and suddenly I was limp from my accusations. It wasn't a matter of my having to say it and then walk away. I was involved with him and his mess. Oh God, Kirkland, clean up all the shit in your head and be *normal*.

His head fell into my lap and I stroked his fine brown hair. I touched a tear that had fallen to his cheek. His hand clutched my arm as he wept. I was half involved with him and half frightened by the power I seemed to have over him.

It went on for several minutes and finally he sat up.

"Nobody," he said slowly, but with affection, "has ever done so much for me."

"Really? Not even Dr. McLeod?"

"No. Not even Dr. McLeod."

"Well," I said, suddenly beginning to snap to. "Let's see the movie."

We stood up and started to walk to the door. He pulled me close to him in front of the full-length mirror and he kissed me.

"Look," he whined as he looked at our reflected images. "You're so much *taller*."

"Yeah," I said, "but you're so much *prettier*."

He laughed and then suggested we play double solitaire. We really didn't want to squirm our way through Bergman.

Rico Vega's class was predictably euphoric. Two hours of teaching, playing, romping, screaming, pretending, and making believe that we were acting. Who could or would dare to ruin this to have us read books, write papers, or learn lines? Who was going to take us out of Ding-Dong Drama and make us agonize a little?

Enter David Hammond. Enter his boots, his flared jeans, his navy turtleneck, his Givenchy scarf, and one decidedly incredible body.

"Oh my God," whispered Leslie, "I think I'm impressed."

"David will take over our class once a week," said Rico. "He's a senior and spent last year studying at the Actor's Studio and has acted professionally."

Let's all hear it for David.

"Okay," said David in a surprisingly low voice. "We're gonna do some exercises to make you more precise . . . accurate . . . in your technique, and if you don't want to do them, you can leave."

We all stayed.

"Okay," he continued, "you two over there."

A meek guy named Jamie and I rose.

"Now you," he said, pointing to Jamie, "tell her all the things you notice about her. And you repeat what he says. . . . Get it?"

"Your sweater is blue."

"Your sweater is blue."

"No, No!" yelled David. "*Your* sweater is blue, damn it, not his."

"Oh," I said nervously. "*My* sweater is blue." I faced Jamie and continued, "My sweater is blue."

"Your eyes are blue," Jamie went on.

I repeated.

"Your hair is brown."

"Goddammit!" shouted David. "What the hell is this? A two-year-old can tell you her fucking hair is brown. Someone else do it."

Another guy, a real wiseass named Michael, sat down across from me.

"Your eyes are two carnivals."

"My eyes are two carnivals?"

"Fuck you, siddown, asshole," said David.

A few people left.

"I'll have to show you myself," he said as he sat down. I panicked.

"You've got a mole on your cheek."

I repeated angrily, barely able to get the words out.

"It's a brown ugly mole."

I repeated.

44

"Your hair needs combing."

My anger rose. I repeated.

"You have a blemish on your chin."

"I have a blemish on my chin," I said, wishing my hair, mole, blemish, and body would disappear from the room.

Definitely a bastard. An egotistical sonofabitch.

"That's it," he said to the few of us who were left.

As I walked out the door, David grabbed my shoulder.

"What's your name, kid?"

"Jane."

"Well, Jane. . . ."

The apology, right?

"Well, Jane," he continued, "going to comb your hair now?"

I ran out the door as if I didn't hear him.

Definitely a bastard.

"Let me take off your sweater," Kirkland breathed.

"No," I said. "I'm cold."

"Damn you. . . . Why do you always wear turtlenecks? Why can't you wear a blouse? Just a nice loose-fitting blouse?"

"Too cold up here. Watch it!"

I sat up. "Do you want to go away next weekend?"

A sigh. "Where?"

"I dunno. New York maybe?"

"Yeah," he said. "I've only been there twice."

"Good. I'll give you a guided tour."

"How do you know New York?" he asked. "And if I

may be so bold . . . how do you know anything?"

"Fuck you, darling."

"No, I mean it. For a country hick you know a hell of a lot. Music, art, antiques, books, movies. Where'dja learn about everything?"

"From the li'l ole cows I'd milk and the roosters when I'd fetch the li'l eggs. Them thar roosters told me all 'bout Bette Davis."

"Them thar roosters don't lay eggs."

"I don't know," I went on. "I'd just learn. It's kind of funny. I never read much except the theater section of *The Times*. Oh, and when I was a kid, I read *The New Yorker*. And I went to New York a lot. I'd go all alone on the train and stay with Anne and Daniel. They're my aunt and uncle . . . the ones who are writers. They'd take me to the theater, the ballet, art galleries, the zoo. And they always, *always* treated me like an adult. They're a little jaded, sometimes annoying, but without them I'd be in Watertown. You're pretty cultured yourself."

"Well," Kirkland said. "My father's family is from South Carolina . . . right out of *Let Us Now Praise Famous Men*. He went to college and to law school and makes a hundred thousand dollars a year. You'd think that would make them socially aware, but I swear that my father licks his dentures after dinner. I mean, he takes them out of his mouth and. . . . Well, I just wandered around Washington and stayed in my room and painted and read and wrote and watched TV. I didn't have an Anne or Daniel. I had these hayseed relatives we never saw and a father who takes out his

46

dentures in public. And I have a mother who belongs to her church women's club and doesn't sleep with my father. I have a brother who's fifteen and on drugs and a baby sister who needs love. And I am eighteen and a half and *I* need love. C'mere."

"When do you want to go to New York? Saturday too late?"

"Skip it. . . ."

How can I explain it? The emphasis at Laurencelle was that everything was crumbling around us. War. Pollution. And why can't we communicate, for Crissake? The government is corrupt. Everyone is getting fucked over all over the world and nobody gives a damn. And nobody listens. And the way the outside world hates us. We take drugs. We're dirty and lazy. And we won't fight wars or cut our hair.

I wasn't too aware of this back in Watertown. Certainly, I thought, some things were unjust. Like my not passing algebra or my bra strap showing at the prom. Otherwise, why would I have chosen to come to Laurencelle in the first place?

Rather than all this moving me out of the dorm and into the streets, I was more content to stay with Kirkland. I'd rather exchange Debbieisms (a game in which we thought of the funniest, rottenest things to say about my roommate) and talk about Vermeer or the most beautiful thing Kirkland had ever drawn or the dumbest thing I ever said.

I'd rather buy bagels in Montpelier for Kirkland and me than contribute to some black kid's bail.

I'd rather walk to a nearby deserted farmhouse than

down Pennsylvania Avenue.

But damned if anyone noticed. It was so taken for granted that we were all radicals that no one really knew just how apathetic I was.

The reason was that for all the air pollution, war, and general fucked-overness, I was very, very happy.

It was time to figure out what the hell was wrong with Moby Dick . . . the great white whale in the sea of psychology books in my room.

In two months Debbie had not cracked once. She had all of her classes either early in the morning while I was sleeping or at night when I'd be out with Kirkland, making fun of her.

All I knew was that she never went out, went home often (a ten-hour busride), kept cookies under her bed, smelled, never undressed in front of me, read, and did term papers for three psych courses including a small group workshop, and that she hated me.

She also had one or two dress days a week. She'd get out her best Lane Bryant, her girdle (size G for Gigantic), heels, a fall, and her Max Factor make-up kit, and play dress-up. Then she'd never leave the room. She'd just sit, all dressed up, reading Carl Rogers until bedtime.

So I decided to corner her one night, which was difficult since she usually cornered *me*. She was lying on her bed, reading *Being and Time* and loudly eating an apple.

"How're your classes going?" I asked.

"Fine."

"Good. . . . You like it here?"

"Yes."

"Did you really want to go here?" I asked stupidly. "I mean, was this where you really wanted to go to college?"

She finally looked up. "Yes."

"Didn't you apply anywhere else?"

"Yes. NYU, Sarah Lawrence, Brandeis, University of Chicago, and Stanford."

"What happened?"

"I got into all of them. What about you?"

"I wanted to come here since I was fourteen. I got into a couple of other schools." I was embarrassed by the fact that the "other schools" were small Midwestern colleges with compulsory squaredancing.

"Is this place a letdown after high school?" she asked.

"You've got to be kidding. I told you I hated it. How about you?"

"Well," she said slowly, "I can't really say. I only went to high school for about a year."

"What happened then?"

"I dropped out when I was fifteen. I'd already skipped a year of school and I despised high school. Everyone had it in for me. So, one day I left and never went back."

I was still as a corpse as she continued.

"I had a teacher from Newark State tutor me for a while and took the state equivalency test. I finished high school in less than two years."

"What are you? A genius?"

"Yes."

She bit into her apple and went back to her book.

I was getting to be the best. The best of everything. I was the most creative drama student . . . old "Freak-'em-out" Potterman used to be absolutely clever without being icky in our improvisations.

Then I would be absolutely *the* most compassionate social psychologist in Modern Problems when someone had a (choose one) parental, emotional, sexual, academic problem. I would tilt my head to one side, lower my voice one compassionate octave, and tell them to shape up.

And being a genius in my Problems of Ed course took little more than finding variations on the "No more pencils, no more books/ No more teacher's dirty looks" theme. It was a matter of having gone through high school, hating it, and then living out my fantasies on changing it.

But a Laurencelle College program does not end there. There is a community commitment. That is, five hours a week (optional, of course) spent serving mankind in the "real world." Almost nobody does this, of course, except an overly anxious altruistic showoff like myself who really revels in cutting out goblins for a Hallowe'en party for orphans . . . or who sits patiently while a senile woman slobbers her problems in a state mental institution . . . or encourages a cripple to walk, as if I were St. Bernadette. All with my head tilted to one side, my eyes fixed attentively on the learning experience (whatever it might be), and playing Eleanor Roosevelt to the social problems of our time.

From Debbie's diary:

Dear Diary:
There can be no doubt that Vermont is the North Pole. I am freezing. Everything is now frozen solid.
Speaking of frozen, my relationship with Jane is still barely tolerable and I wish that she would find another place to live even if it is more than halfway through the semester. Maybe she could work something out with Leslie Shapiro, that Jewish whore from Short Hills. I think that Jane just hangs around her to make herself look like she's in the same league. Enough of this insight crap.
Damn this school! Damn Jane! Damn Eric. He talks to me, but nothing. I love him.

Debbie

"How was your Thanksgiving?" I asked.
Kirkland leaned back in the chair at my desk.
"Dreadful. Uncle Norm. I mean, *Norm,* the one I told you about who teaches history . . . and my little cousins, Robbie and Burton, and my *Grand*mother! Oh Jesus!"
"How are your parents?"
"Insane as usual. My mother. . . . Oh! I've got to

tell you this. My mother gave me the third-degree about you."

"Oh yeah? What did she say?"

"Well, I mean there was no stopping her after she found out you were Jewish. 'They smell, dear. It's common knowledge.' And then she told me I'm beginning to smell. Do you make the obvious connection?"

"Yeah. Did she recognize the odor? Gefilte fish. I've noticed that a lot, Kirkland. You smell like a delicatessen. God, I can't believe your family. Is she that way, really?"

"Do I?"

"Do you what?"

"Smell?"

"No, for Crissake." I said. "What else did she say?"

"You know. The usual. That the Jews had smaller brains than other people. Oh. Sorry. And that you were one cut above niggers. That sort of garbage. 'It's common knowledge, dear, common knowledge.'"

"And did she ask you what our relationship was?" I asked.

"Yeah. I just said you were this girl."

"And?"

"And that's all."

He swiveled around in the chair, looked hard at me for a few seconds.

"Did your mother ask about me?"

"Yes," I said, "one question."

"What was that?"

"She asked me if I loved you."

52

"What did you tell her?"
"Yes. I told her yes."

> "I feel it is the duty of every non-virgin to help another member of his species overcome the state of virginity. . . ."
>
> LESLIE SHAPIRO

"Whaddya wanna know?" she asked.

"I want to know, Leslie, is it possible, I mean, can you, or, I mean, can *I*, really go through this thing without it being an absolute trauma?"

"Look," Leslie said solemnly, "it *may* make a difference. It *may* bother you when it first happens. But not for more than five minutes. I am not responsible for more than five minutes of guilt when you and Kirkland fuck."

I'd read all the Margaret Mead books about the aunts in the tribe preparing the young maidens for the tribal rites. So this was the coming of age at Laurencelle? A Jewish girl from Paramus, New Jersey, instructs her classmate in how to handle the aftershock. "You do this big Israeli folkdance down to the shrink, you see. . . ."

"Jane," Leslie continued, "I don't know why the hell I bother. You and Kirkland have already taken all the animalism out of it. Talk, talk, talk. . . . It's ridiculous."

"Why shouldn't we discuss it before we do it?"

"Because it's not going to make any difference *after* you do it."

"What she wants, if you want to take it from me, is to have you drag her into the woods and fuck the shit out of her."

JOHN PILKINGTON, PH.D.

"That's what he said," Kirkland announced over the phone. "I told you he was a great counselor."

"But he doesn't even know me."

"He knows women."

"He's crazy . . . even for a Ph.D. in psych. He's nuts."

"Look, that's really it, kid. He knows all about instinct, and crap like morals doesn't even enter into it for him. He's basic. He gets right to the problem."

"Problem?"

"Yeah," Kirkland said hesitating, "your—problem. Face it, he's right. Your head is just telling you not to do something you want to do."

"Oh."

"So Jack said for you to listen to your instincts and just . . . do it. You really want to, you know."

"Oh."

"Aw, c'mon, Jane."

KIRKLAND CHAPIN

"It's not that I don't know how to talk to you, Jane. It's just that I'm so stoned right now," Debbie said as she stared out of the window.

"Really?" I asked. "You?"

54

"Yeah. Me. Just smoked down in Jed and Cathy's room."

"How come?"

"I was at an encounter group thing and they asked me. It's the social thing to do."

She giggled. "Debbie the Deb. The soc-i-all thing TO do."

"Sonofabitch," I thought. "The trained bear is making friends. Did the freaks lay it on for her physical appearance? Or did she take the whimpering little ones and let them snuggle up to her mammoth breasts while she played Mama?"

"I like people and people like me," she half sang, half mumbled.

"Huh?"

"I'm a people, Janie." She had never called me Janie before. "I'm a people. You're a people. People are friendly. dot, dot, dot, therefore. . . . That's math, by the way, dot, dot, dot, we are friends. You and me of the harsh glances and the flared-nostril society of Milton House, Room 9, are hereby declared friends."

A snowstorm descended on the campus the first Saturday night in December. No one, it seemed, was going to frolic or in some other way try to live with it. Debbie was in New Jersey for the weekend.

Kirkland sat in my room, listening to his album of Gregorian chants on Debbie's stereo. It was midnight and there were no other sounds or people anywhere near us.

"It's time we slept together," he said. "Jack said it's

time. He said that weeks ago. I want to sleep with you."

He paused and then started to undress.

"All right. All right."

"You *mean* . . ." he beamed like a six-year old.

"I don't want to fight it."

"Well, that's the most passionate thing you've said in a long time."

"I mean, I don't want to be held responsible for your needing four more years of analysis. I don't want you to hate me. I don't want Jack to hate me. The whole goddamn school is going to hate me, I get the feeling. So let's go. Don't discuss it any more. You win. Jack wins. Leslie wins. The college wins. It's Fallen Angel time."

"Shut up." He continued to undress. I removed my flannel nightgown and got into my bed. The room was freezing.

"Jane . . . I want you to know how much I appreciate this. . . ." He came toward the bed. I tried to look away from his chalky-white body.

If Kirkland thought Vermont was cold that evening, he could have grown a palm tree outside compared with his trying to make love to me. What kind of a boy goes ahead and tries with a girl who tells him she'll sleep with him because she's tired of arguing? Kirkland. What kind of a girl realizes that she's doing the last great favor in the life of a total loser? Me.

"Why are you just lying there?"

"It seemed like a good position. . . . Actually I'm

lying here for you."

"Jesus Christ."

"Look, I know you're probably freezing your ass off, so why don't you just get into bed?"

"Yes."

"What's with you tonight?"

"I'm horny."

"I'm Aries."

He laughed and then kissed me.

"Virgo," he whispered as he turned off the desk lamp.

The wind blew through the crack in the window and the Gregorian chants continued. Kirkland was in his moaning-and-groaning stage and I paid little attention. I now could believe the power of passion. He completely ignored the fact that it was little more than a visit to the doctor for me. Any minute he would be "killing two birds with one. . . ."

He sat up quickly and groped his way to my desk.

"Where's the Kleenex? Where's the goddamn Kleenex?"

I sat up and snapped on the desk lamp. I wanted to say, "Nice going!" or some equally snide thing, but I felt nothing but relief.

"Damn . . . damn . . . damn!"

I started to get dressed. As I put on my coat he turned toward me. Tears were running down his cheeks as his skinny white body trembled.

"Not with a bang but with a whimper," I muttered. He didn't hear me.

"Where are you going?"

"I'll do it for you. I'm going for a walk in the snow."

He turned toward the window and slurped as I walked out the door.

I walked into Leslie's room after brunch the next morning.

"Well?" she beamed.

"Well, nothing, except for two frostbitten toes and possible pneumonia."

"Not even possible pregnancy?"

"I doubt if Kirkland's pregnant."

"Jane, goddamnit, what happened last night?"

I told her. She laughed and then turned toward me knowingly.

"Okay. So he was a little too excited. That could only happen to him. And you. But you can try again."

"I *don't* want to."

"Look. When you fall off a horse, you're supposed to. . . ."

"I *don't* want to."

"But, Jane. . . ."

"Look. I didn't want to last night. It's not his problem. It's not mine. I don't like him. I don't like to look at him. I don't like Gregorian chants. I don't like his Sandra Dee voice. I don't like *him*. I don't think I'm afraid of sex. I would love sex . . . just like you. He just turns me off."

I walked out of Leslie's room and trudged through the new snow and back to my room and read one hundred and eighty-seven pages of psychology for the next day's class. I was going to be the only one to have read the assignment and Marion would love me.

I had looked forward to love for at least the past four or five years. It was, of course, supposed to enter my life with violins and harps and flutes. I like flutes, so love must come with flutes. Now I realize it doesn't even come with an accordian.

It was three weeks before the end of the semester when I decided to write off Kirkland permanently. We were silently eating our dessert one cold evening in the dining room.

"What's in this *pie?*" he asked.

"Four and twenty blackbirds?"

"I think they were here, but they left." Pause. "Do you still love me?"

He put down his skimmed milk and looked down at the table.

"Jane. You're acting, well, bitchy?"

"Kirkland. . . ."

"No, really. What's the matter? Tell me."

"Let's walk to your room."

A moment and an interminable silence later we sat facing each other, I on Roger's bed, pulling his goose-down quilt over my legs, then quickly removing it so I'd be able to make a fast getaway.

"Well?" he asked, barely audibly.

"I don't."

"You don't *what?*"

"I-don't-love-you." Quickly I added, "ANY MORE."
Another silence.

"Did you ever really love me?"

"Yes, I think so."

"When?"

"Christ, I don't know."

Tears were approaching his cheeks.

"Did I do something wrong *recently?*"

"Yes."

"What?"

"God, I don't know."

More tears as he stared at the floor and then at me. "You just made me think you loved me. You never cared."

"That's bullshit and you know it. It's not every girl at this asylum who would nurse you through all your diseases, both real and imagined."

"Well, then, just how much do I owe you, nurse?"

"Cut the crap."

"No, I mean it. Well, what a nice little hypocrite you turned out to be. First you wanted. . . ."

I cut in. "*Nothing.* Not a goddamn thing, thank you. Not your illnesses, not your hangups, traumas, allergies, hemorrhoids, or . . ." I paused and said faintly, "you."

"I see, I see," he said softly as he wiped his cheek with his sleeve.

"Here, in your room, it's all right. We can talk, we can laugh, and I enjoy you. But, God, Kirkland, I can't stand *being* with you any more. I get tense and I can't stand facing all the people with you. Because you hate them and they know it. I'm beginning to feel like Mrs.

60

Jack the Ripper. I can't help it. For three months we've been running scared. We're both afraid that somebody, everybody out there is gonna eat us up. And so you dodge behind me. Yet I get sick of being with you. Fuck. . . . I can't make myself clear. I don't love you."

He sobbed for five minutes, and I sat very straight, cross-legged on Roger's bed. He wasn't fighting back but giving out great painful moans. He needed no more ammunition, but I just wanted very suddenly to attack. I was hot and suddenly the accusations spat out of my mouth like machine-gun fire.

"You're . . . cynical. And that's not very healthy. You're afraid of anything that might be improper and yet you love to say, 'Isn't this deliciously naughty?' I can't stand your being so . . . so *cavalier*. And I can't stand your prejudices. That fat Jap is really a nice kid. You make fun of blacks, longhairs, shorthairs, promiscuous girls, and especially your imagined fags. Jesus Christ. I mean, really."

He didn't answer.

"As a matter of fact," I continued, "just about the only people you haven't attacked are heterosexual white virgin Jewish girls, of which I am the only one."

"That's not my fault."

"As a matter of fact, it is."

"Look, sweetheart," he said snidely, "there's only one thing I could have altered, if that's what you mean. And you had several chances, all of which you blew. So don't get bitter with *me* about your sexual shortcomings and problems, of which there are many."

"Why, thank you for the Kirkland-Kinsey Report. Doctor, heal thyself."

"There's *nothing* wrong with me, dear," he said, savoring the statement. "You're the one with the fucked-up Puritan ethic."

"No," I shouted angrily. "I just didn't want *you!*"

"Oh, cut it out, Jane. Of course you did. You just are, well . . . frigid."

Then came a long pause while I suddenly started to cry. He looked at his fingernails while I planned strategy . . . a strategy that never came to my mind since Kirkland had just blown it into a million pieces. I couldn't leave. I couldn't think of an honest comeback.

"Kirk?" I said humbly, "what do you think I should do?"

"See a shrink over the Work Term."

"What will he do?"

"Make you see for yourself why you can't make love to a man."

"Maybe I'll go see a shrink in Boston. Yeah. There must be some sort of psychiatric clinic at Harvard."

I rose to leave. I slipped on my ski jacket and Kirkland opened the door. Our eyes met for a second, then fell toward our knees.

"Then you don't love me?" he asked, just to make sure.

"No. Good-bye."

"Good-bye."

The door closed behind me.

What I learned my first semester at Laurencelle College: permanent-press clothes are a necessity; the average student does not use deodorant; lapis is blue; acid is LSD; what marijuana smells like; I hadn't read any Hermann Hesse; Vermeer is wonderful; nobody (almost nobody) knows movie trivia; sex is not dirty; one doesn't use the school laundry; to say "hello" to strangers; no one reads any more; Jean-Claude Van Itallie; Esalen Institute; no one can type; what a bass guitar is; ups; downs; mescaline won't give you a bad trip; dichotomy; cosmic; comics; macrobiotic; Carl Rogers nods his head a lot; you can't get Dr. Pepper in Vermont; some people put sugar on their salads; how to hitch a ride; how to wash bluejeans; Viola Spolin; Nietzsche; netsukes; nutmeg makes you high; I'm not well traveled; people talk dirty; nobody sees American films or Broadway musicals; and I am Somebody.

Winter
1969

WINTER INDEPENDENT STUDY
WORK TERM REPORT

[With Additional Commentary]

I have never lived in a city before or supported myself or had my own apartment. I felt it would be quite
a challenge to go to Boston and mature through the
experience of living on my own. I had no difficulties
finding an inexpensive apartment with another Laurencelle student, Leslie Shapiro.

We lived outside of Boston in Brighton. There were
many other students from Boston schools living in this
area because it is less expensive than Cambridge or

Beacon Hill. This made it more friendly and personal.

[I was scared shitless, in other words, and those "other students" would just as soon spit on me as look at me. In fact, the first day I was in Boston, a guy wearing a BU jacket was walking his German shepherd, which nonchalantly pissed on my foot.]

As our landlady was rather traditional [bitchy and German] my roommate and I were required to spend most of our money on two months' rent in advance and various deposits. Therefore we both needed to find jobs immediately. We heard of a couple of openings and were interviewed and accepted at the Harvard Coop, a large department store in Cambridge where I worked in the book department.

[We also went to work prior to this at a Boston mental hospital, where at the first coffee break on the first day we looked at each other, nodded, and sneaked out. We never went back.]

The Coop, as it is known, caters to Harvard, Radcliffe, and MIT students, and their world was quite different from my own. It was more urban and "uptight." Yet I was pleased to become friends with many of them.

[Wishful thinking and unadulterated bullshit.]

My job consisted of cashiering and returning books to their proper places. [Anywhere they'd fit.] After a while I became fairly efficient and accustomed to the routine. [I finally learned to make change.]

Boston living has its advantages and disadvantages. After a few weeks I started to miss Vermont and Laurencelle. [It must have been eighty below up there anyway, so I must have been crazy. Also, a day did not go by without my seeing at least fifty Laurencelle students anyway. Most of them were panhandling in Harvard Square. Even Marion Lovelace came into the Coop while I was working, threw her arms around me, kissed me, shrieked, and generally made asses of both of us.]

Anyway, I got used to the MTA and was quite able to find my way around Boston. On my days off [when I'd call in sick] I'd go to the Common or the library or the museums.

[Okay, here's what happened: Leslie lasted at the Coop for six days, then quit. She got some money, flew to Chicago for two weeks "to make someone very happy." I was left alone and scared, and one Sunday I found my way to the Gardiner Museum. I sat on the ledge in front of the indoor garden for what seemed like hours. I loved that garden with its marble and flowers that changed from week to week. At that time they were lilies and yellow chrysanthymums. And my mind sort of drifted into all these scenes—getting married there, living there, making a movie there. It wasn't until a nun came up to me and said, "Beautiful, isn't it?" that I left.]

Occasionally I would entertain friends at my apartment, small as it was, and this was a wonderful thing for me.

[Leslie called Nick Peretti person-to-person in Kent, Ohio. His mother gave Nick's number in New York. Kirkland was Nick's roommate in the city and I finally called him. Surprised and led on, especially when I told him I was alone, he got the next flight from New York to Boston and appeared on my doorstep at three A.M.]

I was very comfortable seeing my Laurencelle friends again and we shared our Work Term experiences.

[Before I could ask what he was doing during his Work Term, he was undressed and sitting on my bed. He grabbed me and started to unbutton my nightgown as I asked what he was doing. I fought like hell and tore ass to Leslie's bedroom, where I locked the door and told Kirkland I was exhausted. He fell asleep in my room. Oh, he was clerking in a bank.]

Soon I was familiar with Boston and enjoyed taking friends on tours.

[The Gardiner Museum did not pacify Kirkland's horniness, and as we were walking down Brookline Avenue, he started to complain about all the money he had spent to come to Boston to see me.

"Don't make me feel guilty!" I shouted, as I quickened the pace of my walk.

"You horrible bitch! You led me here all the way from New York, which is not cheap, and you're still too bitchy to compensate for your . . . your unhealthy sexual attitude."

"You pedantic bastard! For your information I took your lousy advice and *went* to a psychiatric clinic two weeks ago. Remember, *you're* the one who advised it. Anyway, he said there was nothing wrong with *me*, dearest, and it was just that I was never attracted to you to begin with. Just because *you* were attracted to *me*, I thought I was supposed to feel the same way. So that is why I simply cannot feel inadequate or guilty."

70

We walked silently to the corner to wait for the bus. I looked at him and he was crying.]

I stayed at the Coop for the entire Work Term and learned what it was like to be self-supporting and independent. Finally, at the end of February, with two months of Boston behind me and four more months at Laurencelle ahead of me, I left.

Jane Potterman

[When Kirkland and I got back to my apartment, the phone was ringing. Leslie called from New Jersey to tell me she was not coming back to Boston but that I could keep her half of the rent.

Meanwhile, Kirkland packed his things and made some excuse about having to leave early. He left. I did not regret my pathetic lie to him about the psychiatrist. It merely put an imaginary period at the end of an imaginary sentence.]

Spring
1969

▄▄▄▄▄▄▄▄▄▄▄▄

Clean-slate time.

My parents drove me back to school to begin the spring semester. They both hated the place so much that my father did not even turn off the engine of the car. He almost didn't stop. I expected him to drive on and I would have to bail out.

I didn't really mean that my parents hated the school for either moral or philosophical reasons. They were either pretty hip to what went on there or they both were turning in very good performances. Actually, I think they didn't want to have to see another rotten report card of mine. This way they could pretend that I was doing great work (well, actually, I was) or even

Phi Beta Kappa. There would be no way to spoil the illusion.

But my mother. My mother with all the comments about not being able to tell the boys from the girls. And my father always getting big yoks from my mother about how he wished he could have the Pill concession.

And above all, for a four-thousand-dollar investment I wasn't living in Harvard Yard. The school looks so shoddy that I almost sympathized with my father who kept asking, "What do they do with all the money?"

So it was in my favor that they didn't stay very long.

Registration somehow reminded me of a boat filled with immigrants from all kinds of weird countries—like Poland or Estonia or Lithuania—all of whom were in steerage. Laurencelle was the Statue of Liberty and we were the huddled masses.

Nobody was happy, mostly because they had just endured a seven-hour drive with their parents. Also, for four thousand dollars a year at least half of them were less than pleased with their room assignments, and I listened to various conversations at the housing desk.

"We could build a lean-to in the woods when the weather gets warmer," one boy said to another.

"Yeah," said the other, "but who wants to live in the woods with two hundred other fucking lean-tos? I'm just not into a Walden trip anymore. I'm into comfort, dig?

"Who's your roommate?" asked one girl of a petite blonde.

"Uh—some chick named Olivia Berglund. Know her?"

"Yeah. She's the suicidal chick who picks her nose and is always hanging around the corners of the library."

"I don't have a room," one girl said to a boy on the stairs to whom she had just introduced herself.

"I have a single," he replied. "Wanna play Harrad Experiment?"

"Fuck off."

"Maybe that's why you don't have a room."

I got Leslie. Or maybe Leslie got me. I knew very well that I had a tough semester ahead of me because she would be having what she laughingly referred to as "Gentlemen Callers." Shy she was not. So I really had a room only on paper. I had the couch in the lounge in reality.

Leslie was already unpacked as I threw my suitcase on top of the unmade bed.

She was cheerful and obviously happy to be back.

She pointed to the window.

"Nice location, huh?"

"A definite improvement. New dorm, new semester, and a new pair of jeans," I said as I unpacked. "Have you seen anyone yet?"

"Roger lives in Royce. Debbie's three doors down. She hasn't got a roommate. She couldn't unless they knocked a wall down."

"Yeah," I said, laughing. Damn, *damn.* I am so un-principled, I thought. Why didn't I tell her to shove it?

"By the way, I haven't seen Kirkland yet," Leslie said, putting her books in the bookcase. "Not that I've gone out of my way or anything."

I then said something that sounded like Shirley Temple rejecting her spinach.

"I don't want to see that bastard ever, EVER again."

"You can't avoid anyone here. It's impossible. You're trapped with him and two hundred and fifty other nuts for four more months. But you don't have to be nice to him. You don't have to nurse him through another attack of botulism. You just blot the ugly memory out, out, OUT."

There was a knock at the door. It was Kirkland. Before he could speak I shouted, "Out, out, OUT!"

"I've got some news for you," announced Kirkland the next day as he stood at my door again.

"Good or bad?"

"Good for me," he said, with the "bad for you" implied.

"Let's hear it."

"I slept with Maxine last night and she said she'd move in with me."

"For once I have no comeback. May I kiss the bride?"

"It was great, really great."

"You were great, really great, or *she* was great, really great?"

He sat down and looked at me smugly.

"Kirkland, I never considered this a contest. If it was,

I concede, but for God's sake, don't expect me to pin a blue ribbon on your mattress."

"You bitch!" he said angrily. "You'll never learn to praise. You'll never learn to appreciate anything."

"Like what?"

"Like my manhood."

"I'll try to restrain myself, Kirkland, but it won't be easy."

"You're just bitter and—jealous."

"Is that so?"

"You're jealous because you wanted what Maxine's got and you didn't get it."

"I didn't want it."

"You just say that. . . ."

"Please leave?" I asked politely.

He did and I spent the next few minutes smirking at the thought of Kirkland getting VD from a pig like Maxine Aronowitz. . . . Getting Maxine pregnant and explaining it to his mother. . . . "Oooohh, Maxine, may I screw you?" . . . "I've written a poem about your pimples, Maxine. I think you'll love it. . . ."

Ahh . . . beginner's luck.

Let me tell you what happens when your roommate is a nymphomaniac.

It works so that three situations, all bad, are available.

One night (this is the first example) Leslie had an "old friend" visiting from Rutgers. I returned from a movie about midnight to find the door locked. This meant either that Leslie was out and had locked the door (very strange, I thought, since neither of us owned a key) or that I was being locked out.

I was being locked out.

Then another night I confronted her in advance. What I got was this:

"When it happens to you. . . ."

"You wouldn't move an inch, Leslie Shapiro."

"Have some sensitivity."

"I want sleep."

"You're bitter because it's not you."

I was bitter because it wasn't me.

Finally, I figured, What the hell. I'll sleep there. I got a key. After all, it *is* my room, right?

I got a lesson in lovemaking I will never forget.

"Did you ever take ALM French?" she asked the West Point cadet, who was breathing heavily.

"Nnoo. No, ma'am. I never did."

"Well, you had to memorize conversations in French. I remember every one of them. Would you like to hear number Eighty-seven B?"

"Of course."

I was finally learning a language in college. She gave every ALM conversation up to 126 C during the semester. Somehow I always managed to whistle "The Marseillaise" at the appropriate time.

After Kirkland and Maxine had established themselves as part of the Young Unmarrieds' Club at Laurencelle, I began to establish myself as Resident Recluse of my dorm.

Leslie managed to spend one day a week at school and the rest of her time as Guest Lecturer in Foreign Languages at Amherst, Brandeis, Harvard, Penn, Yale, and Catholic University of America.

Debbie had established herself as a Jewish Mother-in-residence in the next dorm and was doing SRO business.

I had skillfully managed to schedule myself for classes each weekday and campus jobs (making three hundred salads) all weekend. I also decided to teach a second-grade class "motor skills" eight hours a week.

But the most masochistic thing I could do I did. I signed up for an acting class with three other people, starring David Hammond as the teacher and co-starring Roger, Maxine, John Leever (as the idiot), and myself. Rico was not teaching a theater course that semester and David's was the only one available. So I was called a pig, a shit, meek, timid, bad, and told to "do it over, do it over, do it over." These were the strongest words of encouragement I received.

I also took a film-criticism course that consisted of four senior boys, a teacher with a tic, twenty books to read, forty-two movies to see, and me.

I sat in my room alone and read, listened to the music crashing through the walls, wrote papers, and became depressed. And I was only two weeks into the semester. Some sort of record for depression.

Occasionally Kirkland would come up to my room to give me a progress report. I'd throw him a bone every once in a while by saying things like, "I'm so glad you're doing your thing," or the one he liked to hear best, "I'll bet she enjoys *that!*"

Then Roger started dumping on me. "I only want to be honest with you, but . . ." and I learned I was dishonest, self-conscious, dumb, and my ears stuck out.

School was hard. Damned hard, considering there were no tests or grades. I always had papers to write, books to read, and classes to attend. Where was my head? I was going to this freaky noncompetitive school, and from the time second semester started I knew that I'd been tricked. Somehow I'd been sucked in by the Laurencelle philosophy of self-motivation. Self-motivation equals achievement. By the end of March self-motivation equaled mononucleosis.

I didn't know what to do about the things that were happening around me, either. That was it. They were all happening *around* me and not *to* me. And the harder I worked, the more apart I became. Who really gave a damn what play I was in or what kid brought me a flower when I taught last week?

On the other hand, I also went out of my way to avoid involvement. I was too busy to march against the war in Boston. I kept eating lunch when a kid gave a speech in the dining room about abolishing the school. I just kept hearing the phrase "Because we pretend to be intellectuals, we masturbate with our minds!" Okay.

And individually I didn't care much either. Kirkland could have died of botulism and I would not even have noticed.

And Debbie was just fat, so I couldn't do anything there either.

It wasn't depressing and it wasn't exciting. I wasn't in a social slump (people still talked to me). But (big college revelation) I wasn't happy.

I went to Roger.
"I'm depressed."
"You always want sympathy. God, Jane!"

I went to my counselor.
"I'm depressed."
"What is depression?"

I went to an encounter group. I caught the flu and was suffering as the group spent three hours discussing whether I should be allowed to go to my room and go to sleep. I was needed to listen to *their* problems.

I went to the library to read Pauline Kael one night, and her own brand of bitchiness could not alleviate my misery.

"Do you want half of my Almond Joy?"

"Huh?"

"It's an Almond Joy. Here. There's something cheerful about that name. You take a name like Mounds. I mean, it could be a laxative."

"Besides," I said, "it doesn't have any almonds."

"You're in my film class, aren't you?"

"You're learning something in it, then. I'm not," he said as he relaxed into the chair next to mine.

"What's your name?"

"Nick," he said with a mouthful of mashed coconut.

"You're Jane . . . the former cheerleader for Kirkland Chapin's ulcers."

"He led his own cheers. I worked for the other team."

"Who's that?"

"*Me.*"

He didn't take his eyes off me. He smiled and I smiled. And he had a quality that I had never seen in anyone at Laurencelle before . . . sweetness.

"Oh my God," I muttered. "You're Nick Peretti."

"Oh my God, yes."

"But you lived in New York with. . . ."

"Little Lord Fauntleroy of the famous Vahginia Fauntleroys."

"Right."

"Only, it's not so Vahginia any more, is it?"

"Yes, Virginia . . . Maxine Aronowitz. . . ."

"The kosher pig."

"Not so kosher, Nick. You should hear what Kirkland tells me about her."

"*Tells* you?"

"Like a kid with a good report card."

"Jesus. When I lived with him, all I got was your report card."

"I flunked, huh? Well, that was a *learning experience.* I learned I hated him."

"Why?" Nick asked.

"God . . . I mean, what can you say about a guy who can't go into a city without going into the emergency room of a hospital for 'sudden acute pains about the diaphragm'?"

"He liked you."

"I was funny."

"I know you are. He told me about a few things and I figured you must have quite a sense of humor."

So we talked. We discussed movies and what Nick was doing, would be doing, and had done. We talked about our families, our hangups, Laurencelle (the first loony bin accredited by the New England Association for Accreditation of Colleges and Universities), and Kirkland.

"Why," I asked, "does an eighteen-year-old college freshman waste her time with a boy like that?"

"Because you find someone in a new and insane place, and you can talk and feel comfortable and say you even love that person because everyone else scares you to death. It's nothing to be ashamed of."

I walked back to my dorm slowly after we stopped talking . . . about three A.M. It was snowing and I didn't notice it until much later, when I stared out of my window to watch the sunrise.

"A senior! Wow!"

"Why?" Nick asked coolly. "I got older and eventually they made me a senior. Granted, most of us found better things to do along the way and left, but I just hung on while other students dropped out right and left. Mostly left."

"You've actually been here for three years?"

"No. I used to go to BU but I came here after a year. Now I'm doing my senior thesis."

"On what?"

"Borrowed time. It costs money, which I haven't got, and time, which I also haven't got."

"Why?"

"The draft."

"Oh," I said, and quickly changed the subject. I have never felt comfortable discussing the draft at Laurencelle. It's too real a thing to discuss in a too unreal place.

"Really, what's your thesis about?"

"I have to make a bunch of films. I know it sounds like heresy, but I really am very happy to be doing a lot of work now. I really enjoy it."

"That's not heresy. It's fantastic. God, I really haven't met too many people around here who are committed to doing anything."

"When I was in Boston, I started to see little scenes all over the city and eventually they looked like little movies. So that's what I'm turning them into . . . little movies. I hope someday they'll grow up and be big movies."

"Wow! Like Fellini."

"Please don't think it's crazy to be ambitious, Jane."

"I don't . . . really. I think it's marvelous."

"I just said that because ambition *is* heresy here. But you work hard enough to realize that all we have are our own ambitions and what little things we have to make ourselves happy."

"I'm so happy to hear someone else say that. I also want to be somebody."

"You are . . . you really are. You're really a some-body. Kirkland told me. . . ."

"No, *please* don't bring him into this."

"Okay, but he kind of led me to believe that you knew where it was at just by the things you said to him. I just really dug the way you didn't take any crap from him when you realized that his insanity was going to prevent you from doing things for yourself."

"He told you that?"

"No. I just assumed that's what happened. That was terrific."

"Thank you."

"Okay, let's take our ambitions to the movie. If you're good, I'll let you see it twice."

A senior. . . . WOW!

"Don't you think she's pretty?" Nick asked as he looked across the dining room at a tall blonde.

"Kind of."

"Do you know her name?"

"Myra Fliegelman. You'll have to change it if you're going to put her in movies, Mr. Mayer."

"Has she got star quality?"

"Yeah. Like the big dipper."

Nick let it pass. He was casting Myra for a film he was making that afternoon called *Bubbles,* about a girl who turns guys off with a "Happy Hippo" bubble-pipe. I was also cast . . . Assistant to the Director. We watched a movie one night and in the credits was "Continuity: Jessamine Hill." So I was called a Continuity Girl. ("But I promise not to call you 'Cont' for short," Nick told me.)

"Do you have the soap and bubblepipe?"

"Right here, Nick. . . . Here, Myra."

"Okay. Write down the F-stop. Can you take a light reading? *Please* remind me to wind the goddamn camera. Okay. Let's go."

The life of a Continuity Girl isn't an easy one.

The first thing I noticed about Nick's room when I saw it for the first time was that it did not look like any other room at Laurencelle.

It definitely was a dorm room. But there was a terrific Victorian table and only one bed. He had a single because he was a senior. On the wall were theater posters for obscure shows I had also loved and hundreds of film books that I had always wanted but could never afford.

The most consistent thing that amazed me about being there was being there. I had known Nick for two weeks and had never seen his room except from the outside. I would go outside his dorm (right next to my dorm) and look up to his window and see if his light was on. I don't know why I really bothered. It was some kind of Romeo and Juliet perversion. It was very teen-age.

Finally, he asked me to come over to see a film he had made the year before which he was showing on his wall. He told me it was very important that I see it.

"Ready?" he asked.

"Okay, hit it, De Mille."

Scene one: A boy in bed. He rises, looks perplexed.

Scene two: A girl (a young innocent named Margie Hagan, whom I knew from my psych class) walking along a garden.

Scene three: (flashback) Three little boys shooting slingshots at paper airplanes.

Scene four: Margie and the boy walking hand in hand in garden.

Scene five: Boy strangles girl.

Scene six: Same as scene one.

All of this had a dismal piano soundtrack.

"Huh?" I said as he turned on the lights.

"Huh, yourself. I'm running it again til you understand it," he said, laughing.

He wasn't kidding. What was he trying to tell me?

"It's important that you understand this," he kept saying.

I was so bored by the sixth showing that I said I *did* understand it, and by praising it, I somehow managed to avoid having to explain it.

But it was not the last time I saw the film.

The road to Laurencelle is paved with good intentions and bills for tuition.

It isn't cheap, and for all the expense I got two things: a place to sleep in the wilds of Vermont and quiet.

On the way up to Laurencelle, before Debbie and Kirkland and Nick, I wondered—no, I *knew*—that I was going to make it worth it. My parents aren't exactly beggars, but they really couldn't afford this school. But they never stopped me and I always liked to think that they never *could* stop me.

So I thought that I would do many things to make good their investment. First, I would learn to be a good student and pursue noble subjects like science and literature. I didn't. Second, I decided not to experiment with drugs. Strike two. I smoked marijuana on several occasions but never felt guilty because I never got stoned. Third, I would never put my social life above my academic life. That's three out of three, as has previously been proven.

So, what were my parents getting for their four-thousand-dollar investment? A pothead? Decidedly not. A loser? No. I just somehow sensed that it was worth it.

I wasn't really with it. I mean, I *felt* with it, but I wasn't. I felt happy and I was.

I looked around and I listened. What was everyone talking about? Emptiness, that's what. Prefacing every statement with "I feel. . . ." (*I* just did that so I don't want to say it's not a valid thing to do.) They would fill in the blank with "lonely," "forgotten," "bored," "numb." And they dug it in a creepy kind of way. Dig the void.

Not Nick and me. It was always a matter of making complete statements. Finishing, starting, finishing. And it wasn't halfassed like everything else at the school. Although I'd been there for a while, I still couldn't adjust to the lack of commitment, motivation, and general inactivity. All of this was excused in the name of learning experience and "getting your head together." I wished these numb and crazy people would stop talking and start doing.

And damned if what I was doing wasn't important! I never thought about it—or tried not to. Wasn't life supposed to be where you loved what you were doing?

Weren't you supposed to get rid of all the bogeymen of arithmetic and verb conjugations someday so you could be free, free, free? And *that* was the sheer delight of being at Laurencelle College.

My school had no traditions. No statues to kiss, no seniors to worship, other than Nick. (I usually never knew exactly who *was* a senior.) And no famous or wealthy alumni. I imagine that if there *were* any famous alumni, they'd disclaim the fact that they ever went to Laurencelle.

At Christmas my friends from home had told me hair-raising stories about panty-raids, beanies, and freshman parades. I had told them about no exams, no grades, never calling a teacher by anything other than his first name, and being able (if one so desired in December) to go to dinner barefoot. I handled myself beautifully, actually, and made everyone feel quite ridiculous for tolerating anything less than my idyllic situation.

Sometimes, though, I would think how terrific it would be to establish some *anti*-traditions. I thought that my school needed a motto. Like "Veritas." If Laurencelle had one, I think it would be "Ignorance Is Bliss."

But with the coming of spring, there were some rituals. On Easter Sunday there was a spontaneous flute concert on the roof of my dorm, followed by an egg hunt and kiteflying. It just happened.

One night during the winter everyone was feeling kind of giddy (or stoned) and all three hundred of us arrived at dinner in greaser attire. (Greaser: a fifties hood whom your mother wouldn't let you go out with unless you were one, in which case I wouldn't know you because my mother never let me go out with people like you.)

So, there were times that were really extraordinary, regardless of how they happened. And I secretly hoped that the extraordinary things would become a tradition.

At exactly midnight the phone in my dorm rang. And at midnight, although everyone was awake, I didn't exactly have to compete for the privilege of answering it.

"I knew it was you!" I said breathlessly because I *did* know it was Nick.

"How?"

"Because I figured your film would come back from being processed today and you'd like to wait to edit it early tomorrow when you're fully awake but you can't wait and you don't want to be up all night editing alone, so I'll be right over."

"Tell me . . . tell me about something," I said nervously as Nick started cutting his film. God, I was happy.

"I was born poor . . . not too poor . . . that sort of crap?"

"Yeah. The maudlin *As the World Turns* stuff."

"You asked for it. Ohio."

"I know that."

"And my father died when I was entering kindergarten. But I told you that. And I fell out of a tree once when I was ten and broke my arm. My mother wanted last rights said while I was having my arm set."

"Really?"

"There. I've just told you *two* things."

"That you're Catholic and your mother's nuts?"

"Wrong. That *I'm* nuts and my *mother's* Catholic."

"I didn't mean to be nosy. Really. I didn't mean to turn it into an encounter group."

"No. That's okay. I don't mind telling you because I'm pretty average for Laurencelle. Nothing that would send you running out of here with your hand over your mouth. That is, unless I told you about my mother's ravioli. *That* would make you sick. I know from experience."

He ran the film. There was Myra, blowing bubbles. "Not bad, but her pimples show up."

"What pimples?" Nick asked. "I think she photographs well."

"It's not a bad film." But it was and he wasn't satisfied.

When we walked out of the editing room, the sun started to appear over the hills and as we walked toward the dorm we talked about how still and beautiful everything was and how glad we were that we could witness Laurencelle with this calm.

Suddenly four or five freaks came running toward us . . . all of them dressed in black with black capes.

They grabbed me and forced me to come with them to the meadow behind the school.

Nick didn't take any of this seriously until he saw

them tie me to a tree. He walked up to one of them who was chanting in front of me.

"Allen, what in *hell* do you want with her?"

"It's Black Sabbath and we need a sacrificial virgin," he replied.

Shit, I thought, does he have to advertise?

"C'mon, Jane, let them sacrifice someone else," Nick said as he untied me.

"Bye, Allen, George, Del. . . ."

We started walking back to the dorm again with that "Ho-hum, another day at Laurencelle" attitude.

"Well," I said, "Lancelot."

"No," he said, "I don't lancelot. Only for you. The other girls couldn't meet their qualifications."

I cringed. Nick saw a six-pack of beer hanging outside someone's window to cool, climbed up, and grabbed it. We then sat on top of the roof of Fisher House and got plastered before the rest of the school had even gotten out of bed.

In the college identity war there are no winners. Maybe, if you're lucky, you get a "positive image of self," but it's usually false. Maybe you see the light, realize you're dumb, ugly, or worthless, but then where are you? So every day I thanked God that I didn't know where it was at. The truth might have destroyed me.

I wondered a lot, though, why people bothered with me. Like Nick. Because I didn't really search for the truth about myself, I could blame it on anything. Like beauty . . . inner, outer, spiritual, physical. Or intelligence. I realized that at Laurencelle I could get away with not knowing about Nietzsche or Dante. A little bit of trivial knowledge begins more conversations than doctoral dissertation on Sartre ever could. The best thing was that I could tell myself that Nick needed me. I could pretend to be his personal oasis in this experimental desert.

Kirkland came up to my room one night to give me the latest news bulletin.

"Well," I said approvingly, "seems like Fibber Mcgee and Molly are going to have their option picked up for next week."

"Stop acting like such a spinster. You're just being shitty because Nick hasn't made it with you."

"Shut up, Kirk."

"It's Kirkland, you bitch, and you know you can't be secretive about these things around here. But you're such an incurable romantic. . . . Don't you realize there's a whole school looking on?"

"Fuck 'em," I said. "Somebody sweeps me off my size-ten feet and everyone wants details."

"There are no details. But if there are, then you can have Nick make a movie of it called *Gidget Goes Astray.*"

"Look, night after night people indiscriminately crawl into bed with strangers. I don't know why I have to defend my position. I don't know why the fuck I'm even talking to you, if you want to know the truth . . . and *I* have to defend my friendship with Nick? That's insane."

"Not here it isn't. If there's one thing I've learned

around here, it's that we're all better off with strangers."

"Yeah. That's it. Everyone sleeps with strangers and then needs five years of analysis to figure out why they can't maintain decent relationships."

"Ah, c'mon," he shrieked, as only Kirkland could shriek. "Stop playing Doris Day Goes to College. With Nick . . . it's like you're a dog chasing a car. Either you'll never catch up or you'll get run over. Yuck. But it's a good metaphor, if I say so myself."

He left. Anyone who sleeps with Maxine Aronowitz has no damn right to call anyone else a dog.

By the end of March something inside me began to become very desperate. And so I worked harder to take the edge off of Laurencelle. I did not allow myself a free moment, and each evening after dinner I'd help Nick edit his films just to be with him and then go back to my room and read until early morning.

"You're not freaking out," Leslie told me. "You're freaking *in*. A freak-out is healthy. You get out of your mess. Freaking in is when you make a bigger mess in the same place."

"What mess?"

"You . . . you work too much."

"I enjoy it. I love it . . . all of it."

"Take it from the top. How about teaching those monsters new math?"

"I can't even teach them old math, but I love it.

"David Hammond."

"There is nothing I can say that will make any sense when it comes to why I go. Maybe because I trust him and he's being a bastard for a good reason. I love it."

"Film class."

"I love it."

"Education class."

"I love it."

"Nick Peretti."

"I love . . . it."

"It's not the same thing."

"No, it's not. He's a human being. Everything else is for credit."

"You're attacking Nick like you attack all of your other work . . . like Joan of Arc. 'I'd like to go to Boston this weekend, but I must study my John Dewey.' Why don't you screw around for a change?"

"Look," I said, "I never, ever enjoyed school before this year. I never knew I could love learning. And now I can, so why do I have to run away from it?"

"And why are you running yourself into the ground with Nick?"

"I like it. I'm a masochist, see?"

"It's hopeless. Give up, okay?"

"No. He's tall, dark, handsome, funny, nice, intelligent, and I like spending time with him."

"Well," she continued, "at least make it productive."

"Whaddya mean?"

"Do something. Seduce him."

"*What?*"

"Touch him . . . you know. Like, some night in the editing room get his mind off the movies. Do it."

"Leslie!"

"Has he ever touched you?"

"No. At least not on purpose. But I refuse to go through little Maxine Aronowitz maneuvers to get into bed with him."

"You're a real human, after all."

"Do you know where I'd like to be this time next year?" I asked Nick as we watched the snow fall outside the dining room one day in mid-April.

"Hollywood?"

"No, Jean-Luc, that's where *you* want to be."

"No," he said. "I want to be right here doing a remake of *Nanook of the North*."

"I'd like to be somewhere else. Someplace where it's always warm and there are no students and no freaky people and no radical creeps and no Kirklands, Leslies, or psychiatrists."

"Hollywood."

"No . . . somewhere that doesn't know about encounter groups or speed freaks or acid rock. Or that hasn't heard of 'deviants,' which we all are, or what girl takes which pills, or Hermann Hesse."

"I'd sing 'Over the Rainbow,' but I don't know the tune. But wherever this place is, I'm sure it's closed for the winter."

"What's the alternative?" I asked.

"Well, you get involved here or you go away a lot."

"You can also freak out."

"Can't get credit for it. No, tomorrow I'm flying into civilization for two, count 'em, two weeks."

"Really?" I asked cheerfully, "work, play, or what?"

"Yes."

Comparison was inevitable. Both Nick and Kirkland were boys who took away my time, my thoughts, and in whom I invested a great deal of attention. One had many, many flaws and I saw them immediately. The other had no flaws except that he didn't fall all over me the way the other did.

One hated the college out of fear. The other hated the college because he was too grown up. Like Wendy in *Peter Pan*. One was puny and physically immature. The other was manly and handsome. With one I felt as if I were living in a tunnel and could see the end of our relationship coming closer and closer each day. With the other I was where I was . . . in Vermont in the spring and it seemed eternal and exactly where I wanted to be . . . young, rather than middle-aged.

So it was with great care that I nurtured my relationship with Nick. Although I knew where it was at, it was better, much better, than anything that had ever made itself available to me.

Laurencelle is the orphanage of the freaks of the world. Old women pick up stray cats. Laurencelle picks up stray people.

One evening after dinner Leslie and I picked up Evan Weisbrod, who was fifteen years old. Evan had run away from Passaic, New Jersey, and Leslie, having once visited there, was sympathetic. Evan had heard the great Vermont myth and decided to skip high school and just live in the woods and attend classes.

But it was Sunday night and snowing, so we found an

empty room for Evan. It belonged to Stanley Nathan, a boy I hardly knew. We deposited Evan there at midnight and assured him that Stan would never know.

At four o'clock in the morning Evan arrived at our door, out of breath and with his nose bleeding.

"That, that insane asshole tried to *kill* me!"

"Who?" we asked, wiping the blood off his face.

"That Nathan guy. He pulled me out of his bed and started slamming me against the wall."

"Jesus," Leslie said, "that guy's really freaked out."

"Yeah," Evan continued as he began to calm down. "But all the time he had me by the collar he kept screaming, 'Who are you to Jane Potterman? Who are you to Jane Potterman?'"

There were certain times at school when things would be calm and I'd look out my window and say, "Oh God. . . .

Dear Diary:

Eric . . . Eric . . . Eric . . . Eric. . . . I don't know why you have flipped me out. No one else likes you. Maybe that's why I do.

He has so much money. He takes me places. He makes me feel like, like a Jewish Mother. I am the big J.M. of all time, but thank God I can give him that much.

Eric is dumpy and he limps for some reason. His voice is too loud, and when he talks he insults everyone. I have the highest IQ in the whole school (Alan Walker told me that) and Eric's flipped me out. It's spring. Who cares?

Jane, please return the O'Neill plays you borrowed.

D.

Nick would go to New York at least once a month. He "did a few things," stayed with "friends," and I missed him. I never really knew when to expect him back. Each night I'd run behind his dorm and look up to see if there was a light in his window. Usually he called as soon as he got back and things would be normal again.

Normal was nice. Normal was going to films together and reviewing them for class. ("Did you understand what Fellini meant by that?" "I don't care what they say about Welles. . . . *Touch of Evil* is a piece of shit.")

Normal was shooting at least three usable minutes of film a week, with me taking light readings of rocks, trees, and even Leslie's breasts (for a quickie porno flick).

Normal was always sitting together at dinner (except Wednesday nights, when Nick had dish crew) and I'd get Nick an extra dessert.

Normal was having Nick call me at two A.M. to ask me to help him write a film script, shoot some film, talk, teach me how to load a 16-mm. Bolex, or say, "Thank you."

But not normal (if you'll pardon all of the preceding Charles Schulz metaphors) was when Nick was away. Then I would fantasize great and wonderful things or little absurdities about his having a New York girlfriend. No, that's not at all absurd, I would think. *He'd tell you.*

And yet when he got back, he'd hurry to see me.

WANTED: A FEMALE

FOR

DAVID HAMMOND'S NEW REVUE

AUDITIONS TUES., APRIL 30, 7 P.M., THEATER STUDIO

"Oh, you'd probably have to walk around in boots with a whip," Nick told me.

"Huh?"

"Don't do it. He's a first-class bastard. Anyone who changes his clothes five times a day is not normal."

"I *couldn't* do it. He hates me and I'm not very good, although he hasn't thrown a chair at me in over a week. No, I will not audition for David's revue. I've got a shit-load of work to do . . . that forty-or-more-page film paper, my teaching, learning scenes for Mr. Gentleman Quarterly's class, and helping you. If he wanted me to audition, he'd ask me."

He asked me. It was a "by the way" thing. He didn't ask Maxine Aronowitz. He asked *me.*

I was the fifth person to go into the audition. It was done very professionally. There was a girl at the door taking names, and David shouted, "Next!" once every four minutes, and girls came out saying, "Oh, I just *know* I'll never get the part."

So I figured, what the hell? I'll just go in there and say I got confused. There must have been a mistake. I thought the Hatha Yoga lecture was here. Oh, I'm sorry.

102

Good-bye.

"Jane Potterman!"

I opened the door and was lifted off the floor by David. He twirled me around, gave me a kiss, and asked about my health.

Bullshit, sir. Please have some sensitivity. Just let me hurry and make an ass of myself in front of you as always and all of these people who are judging me, and then let me go back and cry *now* so I can still get some reading done.

"Read this and then go over there and do it."

I did it. Badly.

"No, Janie," David frowned. "Be nervous. She's a wreck, okay?"

"Okay."

I did it. Only something magic happened. David, Rico, everyone laughed.

"Now read this."

I did.

"Okay. Next."

I walked around by the edge of the pine forest for a half-hour. I then returned to the studio and peeked in the window. A very attractive girl, Mandy Altman, was reading. And reading, and reading. God, well, she'll be nice to look at. No, I thought. I should go charging in there and grab that script and say, "Okay, you bastard, this is the new Jane Potterman, STAR, talking and I'm going to read for you now and be great. Maybe. A Helen Hayes! Er, um, Gale Sondergaard?" Oh, Nick. You tried so hard to keep me from doing this to myself.

I should have listened.

My script was in the morning mail. Long live Ruby Keeler.

I ran to call Nick on the phone.

"Who played Jo in the remake of *Little Women?*"

"Ummmm . . . Kirkland Chapin?"

"No," I said, laughing, "c'mon."

"June Allyson?"

"Right. Who starred in *The Great Waltz?*"

"I know this one, believe it or not. Luise Rainer."

"Right. Who is *going* to star in David Hammond's revue?"

"Debbie Goldman?"

"Nope."

"You?"

"Uh-huh."

"You really want to? I can't believe you can get so excited about working for him. He's a cretin, a real asshole. You've told me that yourself."

My enthusiasm dropped.

"Look," I said, "this is what I enjoy, believe it or not, and even if he is a cretin, he knows what he's doing."

"Have fun," Nick said, not quite understanding that I had hoped he might share my enthusiasm.

"Yeah, I will."

"Well, I have a lot of work to do so. . . ."

"See you in class."

"Yeah, 'bye."

Okay, I thought. Then if it's just going to be a matter of Jane impressing Jane, then so it will be.

* * *

"It's a circus," Nick said as he looked around the dining room. "It looks like the central casting office for a sideshow."

He ran his fingers through his longish black hair and then started playing with the salt shaker.

"Why did you transfer here? You like the city. BU must have had something in it you liked."

"I was different then. I was a commie, hippie, freak, drug addict, revolutionary pervert then."

"Huh?"

"Really. I used to go to Boston Common and smoke dope and plan revolutions."

"What happened?" I asked.

"I came here because all the revolution was over for me. I figured, 'Wow, now Nick can really *do* something to change the fucked-up world.' But here. God. It's all done. Utopia."

"You don't believe that."

"Yeah, I do. I went through a couple of years dropping acid, sitting in dark, dirty apartments, reading Marx, and getting pissed-off. Now, I make movies and don't get pissed-off. The only thing that pisses me off at all is watching everyone else go through the same thing. I mean, they won't all make movies, but they'll become absorbed in something else."

"Why didn't you stay at BU?"

"Did you ever hear a slobbering old . . . I mean *really* old . . . man give a philosophy lecture to five hundred students? Most of them were asleep. And this guy would slurp his way through a lecture and wipe his nose on his hand and everyone would laugh. He didn't even know why, poor slob. And he would just give the lecture, calling us 'young people' and telling us 'what you are about to be you are now becoming.' You just can't take too much of that seriously. Not when a famous professor doesn't know enough to use a handkerchief."

"I love you, Jane. . . . I have always loved you. Will you move in with me?"

Eric walked beside me on my way to the library. Debbie was right. He did limp.

"Well?"

I stopped and almost laughed. If only I didn't hate him so much. . . .

"Eric," I started to say, "Debbie is a friend. . . ."

"So?" He grabbed my arm.

"Debbie," I continued.

"Debbie *what?*"

"Debbie needs someone."

"What does that have to do with me? What does that have to do with anything at all? If I had never met Debbie, then I would never have known you. Thank you, Debbie Goldman! Now will you move in with me?"

"No."

"No *what?*"

"No, for Crissakes. . . ."

It was quite a surprise.

❖   ❖   ❖

I didn't lose track of Kirkland. He somewhere had gotten rid of Maxine and had started to share his room with a rather attractive little pill-popper named Mo.

"Is that like in Curley, Larry, and?" I asked him when he told me in the library.

"Yeah," he said laughing. I didn't expect that.

"She's very dumb, loves sex, very pretty, extremely screwed-up, and rich."

"That's nice. I hope you're both happy."

"We are. Listen, you don't sound so bitchy."

"Should I?"

"Yeah. I'm really disappointed in you. Not because you're not bitchy, but because maybe you've stopped being anything."

"Vapid?"

"Maybe. I don't know. You look very pretty today. I like it when you wear a dress."

"I have to go now. I have a rehearsal."

"I know you got the part. I'll make sure that I see it. Sometimes I'm very sorry about the way things worked out, you know, with us."

"Cut the shit."

"And sometimes I'm not."

An actor belongs in a rehearsal the way cream cheese belongs on a bagel. It's the only way in which an actor knows he's an actor.

I was standing in the theater studio (an appropriately gray basement) and having some nice actor conversation with the other cast members when David walked in.

"Okay. We got eleven days to get it together. You know each other. Rico, Scotty, old Dick the Prick here, and Janie, who just joined us. And this is Roger, who'll be busting his ass as stage manager. There'll be no fucking around. Rehearsals will be here every night at seven until God knows when, and we're all gonna work. You gotta know your lines by tomorrow . . . all of them. Any questions? Let's go."

I loved it. I was the only girl and the guys treated me like shit (that is, one of them). We would work for two hours on the show without a name. It was a series of blackout scenes that satirized everything from mouthwash to Kafka. And there I would stand, making faces, getting laughs, applause, criticism, and just being part of something with a goal, something that would definitely happen and something that would involve Jane Potterman.

We would break after a couple of hours and go to the coffee shop and sit clustered together as if we were the celebrities in Sardi's and all of the tourists from out of town were staring.

And, if it weren't enough, spring finally came.

"I don't know how Laurencelle can handle you any-more, Janie," said Nick as we walked back to the dorm from film class. "I mean, here you are . . . you wrote the outstanding film paper this week, you get all kinds of praise for your teaching. . . . What was that certificate from the Governor?"

"Just for outstanding volunteer work in the state."

"Yeah . . . and you're the star of David's show. I

mean, where the hell can you go from here?"

"Bellow's Falls, if the buses are running."

"No, I mean it. You're some kind of super whiz kid. You should get outa here."

"Why? This is terrific. Why should I go to a university and *not* get a part and *not* write the best paper?"

"Look, don't give me that crap, Potterman. You're just what the Governor said . . . outstanding . . . whether in this shithole or in Nome, Alaska. You got that?"

I was quiet for a moment and then started to comment about the difficulty of the next film assignment.

"Helen Keller heard better than you!"

"Yooou'lll be SWELL! Yooou'll be Great! Gonna have myst'ry meat on a plate," Nick sang as he dumped the gray meat on my plate in the cafeteria. "It's opening night. Shouldn't you be breaking a leg or something?"

"Never say that to a klutz," I answered.

"Is it going to be good?"

"I don't know."

"Can I see it?"

"No."

As I left the dining room I noticed in my mailbox a long white envelope with just my name typed on the front. Inside was a note informing me that I would receive fifteen hundred dollars toward my tuition next year, primarily because of "high academic achievement."

❀   ❀   ❀

In my room was a vase filled with wildflowers. The note read:

> To Jane . . . Kill'em.
> Debbie and Leslie.

And after I showered, made up, dressed, and *felt* perfect, Roger came to my room and gave me a rose with the note, "A warm hand on your opening. Love, David."

The six of us assembled in David's room, gargled with Listerine, fixed our hair, smiled nervously, bit our nails, and did all the stupid little actor things that just seem to kill time.

We were brilliant. Everyone loved it . . . even David . . . and we were all in love with it and each other.

During the four days it ran, I'd go walking and exploring through the meadows. I'd sit dangling my feet in the brook and read. But it was difficult to concentrate when I thought of the last performance I gave and the one yet to come and how good I was and how good *it* was.

The day after the show closed at Laurencelle I felt positively wrecked. We would still do a couple of performances at some other schools in Vermont, but the truth was that everybody who was going to see me at my school had seen me. Back to being a bit player in the dining-room production of *Marat/Sade*.

"John Leever, please. . . . Hello, John? It's me, Jane. . . . Listen, please tell David that I'm sick today and won't be in class. Yeah. . . . I'm sorry, John. I'll do the scene with you at the next class. 'Bye."

Good. Two extra hours to finish my film paper, education paper, learn that scene, learn a part for the one-act next week, and rest.

There was an angry knock at the door.

"Hi . . . uh, David."

"Heard you were sick. Whatsa matter?"

I lowered my voice and raised my temperature.

"I'm just a little tired. . . . Look, I'm really sorry to miss your class, but I just don't feel too well."

"I'll take you to the infirmary. C'mon."

"David, I really appreciate your concern, but I'll be okay."

"You gotta perform day after tomorrow. Don't be selfish."

"I'm sorry." Oh God, David, I thought. Are you watching the best performance I've ever given or are you trying to make me pay for missing your fucking class?

"Lemme steal some yogurt from the kitchen and then we'll go."

David waited downstairs in the infirmary.

I did the most protesting I had ever done at Laurencelle.

"Please, Mrs. McCloygan, I'm just a little tired. I've done a lot of work lately and I need some sleep. David's just a little concerned, that's all."

"I think you'll stay here and sleep."

"No!" I screamed.

"Yes," she said, patting my hand.

I went downstairs to say good-bye to David.

"They're making me stay here."

"Can I get you anything?"

"If you would, the script to the other play, the film book and my notes on my desk, my ed books next to Leslie's stereo . . . and that's all."

"Forget it," he said, kissing me good-bye. "You'll sleep, damnit, if that bitch has to club you over the head. Now get your ass into bed and good-bye."

Five minutes later I was in bed and Pansy McCloygan, a fat middle-aged redhead, handed me a Librium.

"Now we'll just swallow this but we won't go to sleep yet, okay?"

"Why not?"

"It's only two-thirty in the afternoon."

"Here's another capsule. Swallow, but don't go to sleep yet. It's only four and we'll have to have our dinner first, won't we?"

"Yes."

"Here's another little pill. It's going to be dinnertime soon, so don't drift away. Margaret Culkin will be on duty soon and she'll tell you when to sleep."

Margaret Culkin's nasal voice gave me orders to eat the veal cutlet and take another pill . . . a Seconal

. . . afterward.

"Janie," she said nervously, "I've *got* to go home and feed my cat. I really shouldn't leave you . . . you're our only patient . . . but I *have* to feed my cat. Oh, dear . . . it's raining so hard I hate to go out. But my cat . . . I'll be back in five minutes or so. Don't get up. Oh, dear. . . ."

As she went out the door I rushed out from under the covers, feeling subdued, and went into the nurse's office in hope of calling Leslie to let her know where I was.

NAME: Jane Potterman
SYMPTOMS: Manic-depressive, possible
BREAKDOWN: *Careful*
MEDICATION: Sedation

I very calmly went back to my room, changed into my clothes, and put the Seconal in my pocket. As Miss Culkin's Volkswagen pulled into the driveway, I climbed down the fire escape and ran the full mile back to my dorm in the rain.

No one was around. No Leslie, Debbie, or anyone. I called Nick and he was out.

I locked my door, got into bed, turned off the light, and started to cry uncontrollably.

To my knowledge, the infirmary never looked for me.

Some mid-spring social notes:

* Miss Jane Potterman and Mr. Nicholas Peretti hitched to Burlington for a whole day in the dark. They went

to four movies. Miss Potterman yawned and Mr. Peretti took notes for film class.

* Miss Leslie Shapiro decided to get married to the cadet and do some political organizing in San Francisco. ("Whose politics are you going to organize?" she was asked by her roommate.)

* Miss Deborah Goldman and Mr. Eric Beman embarked on a spring motor trip to Mr. Beman's Pennsylvania farm. When Mr. Beman got out of the car to change a flat tire, he was struck by another car and killed. Miss Goldman was not hurt.

Why Kirkland Chapin came to sit with Nick and me at lunch was unclear (and why I was eating the chicken salad was also unclear). Nick was cool. He always was when anyone interfered in our conversation.

"What are you up to?" Nick asked blandly.

"Sin," Kirkland answered.

"What else is new?" I asked.

"Is *Ray* coming to visit you?" Kirkland asked in a tone I can only describe as the queen who coyly asked the troll, "Well, is your name Rumpelstiltskin?"

I wondered who Ray was.

"He's coming two weeks before the end of the semester. He's staying until I get out and then we are taking off for New York."

Who was Ray?

"And who's visiting *you?*" Nick asked with equal coyness. God, this was getting me down.

"Just . . . well . . . girls."

He took his tray and left.

"God," Nick said shaking his head, "he's the only guy I know who wears his prick on his sleeve."

"Who's Ray?"

Nick answered quickly, "He's a friend of mine from the city . . . a literature teacher at NYU."

"Oh."

"You'll like him . . . he's very funny and a fantastic trivia player."

I made a mental note to arrange my last two weeks of the semester to include, sadly, an extra person.

"You'll really like him," Nick reassured me.

"You thought I was going to commit suicide, didn't you?" asked Debbie as she put down her Buber book.

"No. Not really," I said. "Flip out, maybe, but not kill yourself."

"I wanted to. I know I look like shit, don't have any friends who don't use me, can't shake my parents, and go to a second-rate college, but I have never been better off."

"Huh?"

"I think I come out smelling like a rose."

Not exactly, I thought.

"Really, I look around this place and I realize I'm the smartest one here. No one I've met yet is better informed or more competent. They're all floundering in stupid relationships."

"Like me?"

"Not exactly. You work pretty hard. But I swear to

God, every time you see Nick you react like a cow in heat."

"That's subtle."

"It's true. I have power. People only come to me when they need me. I can be absolutely certain of that."

"What's so terrific about *that?*"

"It stops me from wanting to commit suicide."

The day Ray arrived I was standing behind one of the huge pine trees in front of our dorm. It wasn't Supersleuth or anything. I just wanted to find out what it was all about.

I liked him right away, although I couldn't see him too well. The needles from the pine tree kept getting in my eyes. I also couldn't hear what he was saying to Nick, but they were both talking and making gestures with their hands and laughing wildly as they entered the dorm. It was like a movie without sound. But after three months with Nick everything seemed like a movie. As the door shut behind them I thought, The End . . . five . . . four . . . three . . . two . . . one. And the celluloid whips madly around the reel. The lights come up. Everybody out of the theater.

The question at hand is why did it take me (a) so long to realize what was happening, and (b) so long to accept it?

Every time during the weekend that I ran into Nick and Ray, Ray would be polite and talk and he was genuinely nice. And funny. But somehow Nick would rush him away—to the library, dinner in town, anywhere. And Ray would apologize and leave.

Nick always looked uncomfortable when I sat with them at a concert or film or dinner. He squirmed and was distant.

But the morning of mornings was Monday film class. It was my turn to wake Nick. I would pretend to be fully awake and an explosion of energy, but it was painful that morning when I was so full of questions and anger.

"C'mon, Nick, time to get up."

No answer.

"Hey, Frankie, hey, Annette . . . surf's up!"

I then proceeded to the next plan of getting him up. I tried to open the door, but it was locked. He never locked the door unless he was not in his room.

I started to walk away but I heard people moving, breathing, stretching, and whispering.

"Nick?"

Still no answer.

He did eventually get to class and I didn't even ask whether he had heard me.

The answer to parts (a) and (b) of the question is "Laurencelle College." For all the encounter-I-want-to-get-to-know-the-real-you bullshit, the real *anyone* is pretty hairy. But because we represent the most progressive ideal in education and we've been around and seen so much, nothing is supposed to shock us. It's very Ho-hum, another day in college. Nothing ever shocks us.

There is little to be said after you decide that you are unlucky in love.

I was tired. I couldn't consider spending my time

hanging on to the banister in my nightgown, crying "Oh God!" It wasn't me.

I also couldn't see propositioning guys in the dining room. I wouldn't know how to go about it.

And I don't dig the confessor bit particularly, either. It's not constructive and, besides, damnit, there was not a discreet human being in the entire college.

Back to the banister thing. Maybe I *do* do that. In my head, I mean. And all the time I'm a very stiff-upper-lip-coffee-cup-soap-opera lady. Greer Garson.

Pity . . . not that, either. And there was a lot of that going around in the encounter group circles. I could really cash in. I could be a T-groupie!

There was one constructive way out of this. Work.

Marijuana is supposed to make you calm. It usually does, although I did not smoke often.

"Are you *sure* it won't last too long?" Kirkland drawled as he received the pipe from Roger.

"C'mon," Roger said encouragingly, "take a long deep breath and hold it in."

"Stop coughing," I said after he followed Roger's instructions.

I smoked more that evening than most people usually do. That is, I got my own pipe and made it my exclusive property. A few other kids came in, attracted to the smell, like bees to flowers.

"Fuck you, Kirkland."

"What was that?"

"I said, 'Fuck you.'" I went back to my corner of the room.

"Do I detect some hostility, Miss Potterman?"

"Damn right you do."

"Anything I did lately? I haven't spoken to you for over a month . . . since you went Equity or whatever the hell happened when you became the star of David Hammond's show."

"Not Equity," I said, "royalty."

"Pardon me, Your Majesty."

"Well, you're royalty, too . . . you're raving royalty. You're a bloody *queen*."

"You look, Janie Potterman. I know I'm a little swishy. I know my voice is high. But living with two different girls this semester, quite successfully I might add, does not a queen make. If you want to make a distinction, I suggest that you take a closer look at your matinee idol, Mr. Peretti. He and that friend of his look like two ladies at tea."

"Shut up. Jealous?"

"Roger," Kirkland continued, "tell Jane what you saw today."

"Huh?"

"Nick."

"Oh . . . Nick. Yeah. Kissing like a twelve-year-old in the woods. It was kinda cute until I realized it was a guy."

"You liars! You're so queer you make everyone else look that way!"

"I knew about Nick in New York," Kirkland said. "He went off on weekends to live with Ray. I knew they had something going. Leslie knew it. Jesus! *Everybody* knew it."

"Good thing you didn't get involved," Roger said, inhaling from the pipe.

I ran out of the room, down the stairs, and wildly circled Nick's dorm, screaming and crying.

"Stop it!" Kirkland commanded as he grabbed my arm.

I broke loose and sat under Nick's window as silent tears fell down my cheeks. I talked to the window.

"Make them stop saying that. Make them go away. Come down here, Nick. Make them all go away. Please. When the next person asks me to read his novel or look at his movie or see his paintings, I'm going to tell him it STINKS!"

"You can't go into your room," Kirkland announced as he helped me off the ground.

"Why not?"

"There's some guy in there with Leslie. Come on. I'll let you sleep in my room. Ozzie-and-Harriet style. I promise I won't touch you."

"No."

"I really won't. I promise. I've had girls in there I've touched and screwed and talked with for long, long periods of time and I always wished it was you instead. I really did. But because I did, and I still do, I promise I won't touch you.

I fell asleep next to two rolled-up Japanese prints, a mortar and pestle, a package of Ritz crackers, and Kirkland Chapin.

Thinking about the future gave me a headache. The possibilities were endless: I could be in the Laurencelle reruns the following September. I could, as Kirkland suggested, become a candy striper at the Masters and Johnson clinic. Or, as I finally decided, go away.

Everyone was leaving anyway. Mostly there was going to be a mass migration to California which was supposed to be the ultimate freak-out after Laurencelle. Leslie was going there.

I wondered what happened to the Vermont ideal. All the city kids had tried it and shrugged it off. It didn't fit. Maybe with all the self-involvement they didn't even notice that they were ever there.

How's this for a movie? Still a week to go in the semester and I'm very calm. A friend is a friend, right? So I walked up to Nick's room and I didn't have to knock. The door was open.

The posters were gone. The bed was just a frame and bare mattress. No books. No clothes. Just a few wire hangers in the closet. One empty room. Nick's empty room. The only object in it other than those given to him by the college was the "Happy Hippo" bubble-pipe from the first movie we made. He was definitely gone.

I sat on the desk by the open window and blew bubbles out of it for a few minutes and thought about sad things until I realized the whole scene was contrived. I put the bubblepipe back on his desk and left.

The only reason this would be a bad movie is because it really happened and because somebody I knew had had the nerve to set me up for it.

Debbie was packing her trunks. I didn't even want to *think* about elephants packing their own trunks. She was my friend.

"I came to say good-bye."

She looked up and smiled.

"As you can see," she said, "I'm getting the hell out of here."

"You sound pretty happy to be leaving. It's not *The Group* yet. We've still got three years to go."

"Yeah . . . and already I'm getting nostalgic about this place. Like hating you."

"And hating you."

"And your being in the lounge in the early days . . . like last fall . . . with Kirkland and coming upstairs to slip into something more comfortable . . . like a chastity belt."

"No, actually I waited until you went out so I could read your diary. I haven't read it in a while, though. Did I improve?"

"No," she laughed. "*I* improved. I threw it out."

"I think we're both trying in our own bitchy way to tell each other that we're growing up."

She continued packing her records . . . the old Herbie Mann, Peter, Paul and Mary . . . and her psychology books.

"I have some news. I achieved again." I didn't pause long enough for her to ask what. "I'm going on a Field Study. A federal-grant one. To Hawaii."

The usual round of "Oh, that's fantastic."

"I can't believe how easily things have come to me. It was never like that before. It's all been very, very easy."

"Think back," she said. "The *people* were hard."

I stood up. "Well, it's '*Aloha oe*' time. I'll write a message on a coconut and send it to you. Maybe I'll study the sex life of the breadfruit, just like in *Mutiny on the Bounty*. Maybe I'll. . . ."

I stopped for a second.

"Good-bye, Deb. Take care of yourself."

"Bye."

I walked down the hall. Everyone had left and the only sound I could hear was the click of Debbie's trunk as she closed it.